Problems on Eldora Prime

Book I of the Dragons in Space Series

Sandy Lender

Other Works by Sandy Lender

Choices Meant for Gods—2007
Choices Meant for Kings—2009

What Choices We Made, Vol 1—2008
What Choices We Made, Vol II—2010

"A Legacy Protected," *Winter's Night* Magazine
"Desecrated Ring," Keith Publications Halloween
"Dragons in Crisis," *Winter's Night* Magazine

Advance Praise for
Problems on Eldora Prime

"Sandy Lender's space adventure *Problems on Eldora Prime* is fast-paced and action-filled with villains you will love to hate and heroines and heroes you won't soon forget, especially the spunky pilot Khiry whose indomitable spirit heartens and inspires. *Problems on Eldora Prime* will have young readers on the edge of their seats, holding their breaths until the final page is turned."

–Janie Franz, Midwest Book Reviews, author of *The Bowdancer Saga*

"What a *ride! Problems on Eldora Prime* was one of the best fantasy novels I have ever read—I couldn't put it down. I couldn't wait to find out what would happen to Khiry and her crew—and I absolutely fell in love with the dragons. If you love fantasy or horror, you will love this fast-paced novel by Sandy Lender."

–Greta Gunselman, Timeless-Teens.com

"*Problems on Eldora Prime* is a fast-paced thrill ride of an adventure that is sure to keep even the most reluctant readers engaged."

–Marleen Iffrig, middle school communication arts teacher

"What happens when you take some diced *Jurassic Park* action, fresh bits of *I Am Legend*, a pinch of *Star Trek*, and simmer them in a stock of Sandy Lender's dragon-meets-heroine (the *Choices* series)? You get a wolf-it-down, good-to-the-last-drop page-turner! Well done!"

–Zack Sargent, father of teens

"Life and death. Love and hate. Redemption and treason. *Problems on Eldora Prime* packs them all in…. With the creation of her heroine, Khiry Okerson, author Sandy Lender has proven that she can keep pace with the giants of the genre. The story was so easy and fast-paced, I found myself reading it all in a matter of hours. Three to be exact. Powerful testament to the overall goodness of this book."

–MaryAnn Phillippe, sci-fi/fantasy reader

"Problems on Eldora Prime is perhaps the most inventive science fiction novel I have ever read. Once again, Sandy Lender has reshaped and redefined a genre with her writing and succeeded on every level."

-Jamieson Wolf, author of The Ghost Mirror

Problems on Eldora Prime

Book I of the Dragons in Space Series

Sandy Lender

This is a work of fiction. Names, characters, places, and incidents are products of the author's imagination or are used fictitiously and are not to be construed as real. Any resemblance to actual events, locales, organizations, or persons, living or dead, is entirely coincidental.

Problems on Eldora Prime
Copyright© October 2010 Sandy Lender

ISBN: 978-0-9866406-2-9

Cover Artist: Jamieson Wolf
Text: Sandy Lender
Cover Photo: Dag Seagren

Night Wolf Publications
Where every story has a beginning…
www.nightwolfpublications.com

Problems on Eldora Prime

Book I of the Dragons in Space Series

Sandy Lender

Vocabulary Helps

Language mutates over time in any society. While the adventure in *Problems on Eldora Prime* takes place a mere fifty+ years in our future, the advances in space exploration, the discovery of intelligent life beyond our galaxy, the climate flux on Earth, and the usual addition of words with technology and societal change during those fifty years necessitated some vocabulary "helps" for the reader.

Blender = *n.* a member of the resistance who stays on Earth and "blends" in

Dry = *adj.* not bad (if it's "dry," it's a good situation)

Jump = *v.* leave planet

Jumper = *n.* a member of the resistance who leaves Earth to run errands, recruit

Melon = *n., adj.* idiot, stupid

Mixer = *n.* an Earthling who'll pag or even petition to marry an alien (non-Earthling); at press time, no mixer marriages have been approved by the United Society for Peace and Strength (USPS)

Mixling = *n.* the product of a mixer "relationship;" most mixlings don't survive gestation and Authority refuses to appoint a genetics committee to study the science of saving them

Pag/pagged = *v., n.* screw/screwed (sexual; slightly less offensive than peg)

Peg = *v., n.* frack

Spang/spanged = *v.* shoot/kill with a gun of any kind

Tagger = *n.* mercenary

That's dry = a phrase meaning "that's been lucky so far" or "that's brought good luck"

Tighter = *n.* prostitute

Wetting = *v.* getting bad (if it's "getting wetter," it's getting worse)

Problems on Eldora Prime

Book I of the Dragons in Space Series

Sandy Lender

Chapter One

Khiry slammed both fists down on the metal console in front of her. "Do you want me to fly this thing or not?" she demanded.

Over the chaos of beeps, hissing steam, and an obnoxious wail that sounded like a fire alarm from a school on Earth, Captain Marlon shouted back a tirade with one too many curses about her family. Khiry swiveled her chair with its familiar squeak lost under the cacophony to glare at him. With the welded cockpit windows now to her back, she faced not just the hulking captain, but also his wiry teenage security chief, Gibson. Behind them, the gray and metallic panels of sparking wires and blinking lights reminded her just how many systems on the ship were affected by the strain they experienced.

It smelled like an electrical fire waiting to happen—it didn't bode well for liftoff.

Marlon and his nephew Gibson stood just to the left and maybe two paces behind her station in the shadows cast from equipment and monitors, as if they were afraid of a seventeen-year-old girl. It was about as far as the Instigator's bridge would allow the captain to stand out of reach of either his helmswoman or his marksman. The latter was strangely absent from the even uglier station across from Khiry. Captain Marlon had his own chair directly between the two, complete with a metal board full of switches and gadgets he could swing in and out of his way to play with to his heart's content.

Of course, to sit in the chair would lower him to her level. It would compel him to do something useful. So he stood behind it, hanging onto a handle he'd welded into the ceiling bulkhead panel specifically for this purpose. The weld blended perfectly with the hand-me-down décor of the rest of his flung-together bridge.

It wasn't what you'd call standard USPS-issue material. United Society for Peace and Strength. That's not to say Khiry expected the ship to fall out of the heavens anytime soon; the crew could keep it together well enough. But the Instigator had her share of lightyears and the wear showed—inside and out.

Security Chief Gibson didn't have a seat on the bridge. In fact, he had no business being on the bridge during liftoff. The captain had requested him here today because Kor, the marksman, had yet to arrive.

"You could tell me what the devil's got us so heavy that I can't lift off Eldora Moon, Marlon," Khiry snarled. "How'm I supposed to compensate for—"

"Just compensate as you go," the captain sniped back. His ice-blue eyes flashed with irritation at her. Every Greco-roman feature of his face flared with the same anger she felt, but his perfectly coifed Caesar hair cut remained unruffled. The fine black hair lay exactly where he'd placed and plastered each bit that morning before leaving his second-rate suite on Eldora Moon. If not for the beads of worry-sweat that hung from the ends of the groups of hair, one might think he wore a wig. "Just get us outta here now."

Khiry swung back to face her station, muttering about Marlon's manhood. She wondered just how the engineer, Red, was going to keep the ship together if they lifted off with as much thrust as Marlon demanded of her.

She flipped one of a dozen toggle switches on her console and shouted over the incessant noise. "Red! We've gotta problem!"

"Tell me something I *don't* know," a woman's voice crackled. It was barely audible over a new alarm bell that sounded on Khiry's panel. This one was accompanied by a flashing red light. This one got her attention.

"What the devil does USPS want?" Khiry asked aloud, but asked no one in particular.

"Don't answer that," Marlon commanded.

Khiry shot him an annoyed glance over her shoulder as she returned her attention to the ship's engineer. Raising her voice, she yelled in the direction of the console's mic, "Red, we need more power to get off the ground. Give me anything you've got to hold this baby together."

"You're nuts," the woman called back. "I'll do what I can."

Khiry flipped the toggle switch back to its "off" position. The high-pitched beep, double-beep, beep of the United Society for Peace and Strength's alarm bell rang in again, overpowering a crackle of static that she assumed was some crew member who tried to call the bridge. "I can't ignore the USPS," she said, flipping another toggle switch.

Marlon had already started his protest, and then stopped short as a clean-shaven young man in uniform appeared on one of Khiry's monitors. His gray pointy hat matched his gray eyes and gray disposition and the stark gray walls behind him. "Instigator crew, you are ordered to power down and open your hatch to be boarded by USPS Authority Customs Investigation at once."

"ACI?" Khiry muttered. To the screen she said, "We were given clearance for liftoff not half an hour ago."

She wondered what all the officer could see of their bridge. Could he see the shivering bulkheads and panels with their smoking parts? Or Marlon and Gibson hovering in the background? For that matter, would he request to talk to the captain or the young security chief?

For certain, this officer of her extended government would see her from the little camera mounted in the screen she peered at now. He would see her simple farm-girl features that set so many people at ease, perhaps setting him at ease. He would see her simple brown hair held back by a thin brown headband to keep it out of her face. He would see her doe-brown eyes that peered back at him for simple answers. Like so many people before him, he might be lulled into complacency by her youthful, gentle appearance.

Like so many people before him, he would be duped.

"This is not open for debate," the serious image answered. "You are ordered to power down—"

Marlon's hand struck the toggle switch like a snake attacks a mouse. The image and voice disappeared, and he hissed directly into Khiry's ear, his musty breath overwhelming her, "Get this ship off the ground now or so help me—"

"What's with all the ACI outside?" Kor's voice suddenly demanded. His muscular frame pushed past Gibson as if the security officer were an annoying gnat. "And what's the big idea powering up before I'm on the bridge? You can't just up and leave me, Marlon."

Marlon didn't show relief at the young man's presence, but he brightened at a new prospect. "Kor! Take your station. Power up weapons."

Chapter Two

The youth named Kor dropped a rain-soaked duffle bag with a thud against the metal flooring and shook his wet hair like a bear. When dry, it wouldn't be so black. It would be more of a rich brown with lighter brown chunks streaked through it. Right now, it was almost curly from the soaking he'd gotten outside—the soaking of an Eldora Moon storm that cast a gloom over the already dreary bridge. It brought a cleansing scent like clean linens to the smoky scene.

After he shook, Kor tugged at his cotton t-shirt, letting the wet material hug every definition of muscle in his arms and back, until he had a good wad of it in his hands. He rung it out, getting a pretty good trickle of water to splash to the floor.

Marlon seethed.

Kor looked him dead in the eye. "Now I know you didn't just suggest I power up weapons against the USPS."

"Get your tail in that chair and power up—"

"They're bringing out a phase canon!" Khiry announced. She pointed to the front bank of windows as if no one would know where to look. As if she didn't speak to someone three years her senior, she ordered, "Kor, you better power up something if we're not planning a quick surrender."

"Why are we not off the moon?" Marlon demanded.

"Why are you not telling me what's on board?" she demanded back.

"It's none of your pegging business. Now get us off the ground before I have Trane fire you out the airlock."

Khiry pulled another lever and slammed her hand down on a button with the words "fuel mix" etched below it. "I'll try again. Let's hope we don't shake apart on the platform."

She looked back at Gibson, who cringed as if he'd been hit. For a security chief, he didn't display much bravado clinging to the doorway with white knuckles. He stared wide-eyed out the window as if he expected a plasma bolt to crash through and spang him. Khiry wondered if he was about to run away into the depths of the ship.

Over the complaint of the ship's engines, she heard the familiar whir of the Instigator's phase canon power up. Kor was fast. She spared a glance from her controls to him. The young man's stoic presence set her at ease for some reason.

The high-pitched beep, double beep, beep sounded on Khiry's console. She didn't even glance at the red light this time. Too many fingers were needed to trouble-shoot this lift-off. Better to pretend their communications were down anyway.

"Is that USPS?" Kor asked.

"Mind your business," Marlon snapped. "Target that phase canon. Spang it."

"Aye, Captain. And you'll speak at my trial?"

"We'll get no trials," Khiry muttered under her breath. "This gets wetter by the minute." She knew no good could come of this day.

Whatever her personal opinions on the United Society for Peace and Strength or its Presidente Lamahl Endh back on Earth, she didn't condone treason. To ignore a direct request to power down and submit to an investigation bordered on treason. Spanging an Authority Customs Investigation team? That didn't just *cross* the line. That jumped up and down on the line while thumbing your nose and mooning someone pretty high up the chain of command—possibly Presidente Lamahl Endh himself.

Marlon leaned over her console again. He flipped the switch to speak to Red in engineering. "When you get us enough energy to get off this rock, start fixing things. My ship's falling apart around my ears."

"When?" the tinny female voice sassed back. "You mean *if*, right?"

"Make it happen!" He neglected to flip the toggle back before stepping to his space behind the stations, watching ACI vehicles move toward his vessel.

"Why are we still on the ground?"

As if she heard his furious question, the ship slowly began to rise. She shook and shuddered, screaming and wailing as if every bolt and weld would fly apart from the strain. Despite the thrust of the engines, the rise was maddeningly slow. The ACI vehicles on the moon's surface backed away from the enormous energy and heat. Sound became all anyone knew.

Sound rattled their teeth. Sound joined the shudder of the ship to bang their brains against their skulls. Khiry closed her eyes against the pain of it, praying to God that they'd break atmosphere without falling back to the moon's surface.

"This is gonna be a short trip," she heard Red shout over the communications link.

Another wire sparked nearby, releasing the smell of electric heat.

"We're moving," Marlon shouted.

The incessant beep of the USPS alarm pierced Khiry's brain like a harbinger of bad news. Of all the alarms, buzzers, crackles, and sirens filling the ship, that one high-pitched beep tolled their doom above all the others. She opened her eyes to the light that accompanied it. While there was no more she could do to get the ship out of atmosphere, there was something she could do about the blasted USPS alarm.

She dropped from her chair to duck under her console panel. She fidgeted with a metal plate for only a second before it shook loose for her. She reached up to the wires that lay in perfect order, a direct contrast to just about everything else on the bridge. Selecting the one she needed she yanked once, hard, pulling the wire from its socket. The beep stopped instantly and she sighed in relief.

*   *   *   *   *

It took nearly five minutes to break atmosphere. She couldn't believe they made it. She couldn't believe the Instigator held together. During that five minutes, Marlon had ordered her to pull more wires, silencing more alarms. Hoses still hissed but wires sent out sudden and surprising showers of sparks less frequently. Overall, the ship was quieter, which would make it more challenging to fix.

"They'll send ships after us," Kor said. His moody brown eyes cut through the waning smoke and into her. "Can you get us into hyperdrive?"

"Red?" Khiry asked the air. "Are you still in engineering?"

"Well, I *was* thinking about going into human anatomy fulltime, but, for now, engineering is what I'm best at. Next to sex, of course."

"Red, I'm telling you, USPS is going to spang us out of the heavens. I need some more power to get us into hyperdrive." Choking on the haze in the air undermined the command in her voice. "Can you give it to me?"

Silence answered. Obviously, the bodiless voice from engineering weighed the seriousness of Khiry's question. A sultry, half-moan answered, "I can give it to you, Baby."

Khiry flipped the toggle switch off and turned to Marlon. "Now, you wanna tell me what we just became outlaws for?"

"Mind your business and get us to Earth as fast as—"

"Mind my business? I think it *is* my business when I commit treason for you."

A small voice interrupted then, and all six eyes turned to the bridge's metal doorway. Even though the open doorways on the Instigator were only half a meter wide and just less than two meters tall, the young lady who stood in this one seemed small in comparison.

She had a child actress look about her—sort of a Shirley Temple from the early 1900s on Earth. No one could guess Shayla's true age, and no one had ever bothered to ask. Her eyes were green like a special breed of cat and she slunk like a cat everywhere she went on the ship, as if she always intended to hide from the other crew members. Her pale pretty features shifted to "frightened" when Marlon scowled at her for interrupting a crisis.

"What the devil do you want?"

"Mr. Kent wants to know why he can't get to his luggage. He has valuables he wants to check—"

"Who the devil's Kent?" Marlon groused.

"Paying transport," Khiry supplied.

"Tell him to go to hell," Marlon said.

"Please tell Mr. Kent to be patient," Khiry told Shayla. "We have a situation right now. He should stay in his quarters until someone tells him it's safe to come out. As should you."

Shayla nodded, and then scurried away on silent feet.

Marlon turned on Khiry then. "How many paying transports we got?"

"Seven."

"Make sure they all stay—"

"Yes, you've already told Shayla to keep them all out of the cargo hold. Is that why we had trouble with liftoff? Something in the cargo hold?"

He pointed a finger at her. "Just keep everyone outta there. You, too."

A beep from Khiry's console stopped the conversation. She flipped a switch. "Go, Red."

"You've got what you need. Take us out."

"Fix what else you can next," Khiry ordered.

"I'm not an idiot."

Khiry turned the switch off and pressed new buttons, going through a new sequence for propulsion. She sent a new chemical mix to the engines and pulled a communications device down from its cradle above her head. Its cord expanded to reach her mouth. Pushing a button on its side, she spoke into the receiver. "All hands and transports, the Instigator is preparing to enter hyperdrive. We will accelerate to our optimum speed over the next hour. The initial acceleration may cause some discomfort. Please prepare yourself for the impact on three, two, one."

She released the communications button and pulled a lever for propulsion. It pleased her to see out of her peripheral vision Captain Marlon stumble as the ship jerked into accelerated motion. She heard him mutter a curse in her name, but a smile still played at her lips. She replaced the communications device, letting its cord retract on its own.

"If you've got this thing on a course for Earth, you can go below to help Red," Marlon ordered.

Her smile disappeared.

"You expect me to leave an injured ship on acceleration and autopilot this close to a moon and a planet?" She offered this excuse for her reticence to go to engineering when, in fact, she dreaded being anywhere near the tighter Red.

"Do as you're told."

Gibson finally spoke. "I can watch the controls."

Khiry didn't relish the idea of the sad excuse for a security officer in charge of the ship's controls. He might be a year older than her, but that didn't mean he had skills for the job. "Or you could go help Red," Khiry suggested to him.

Marlon glowered at her, sending her on her way in a huff.

Kor leaned back in his chair, swiveling it around to face the captain and security chief. He draped one muscular arm across his console, the other down the front of his body. No one could mistake him for anything but relaxed and in control. "Why are you on the bridge?" Kor asked Gibson, obviously confronting an inferior being.

"Captain asked me to be here because we couldn't find you."

"Yes, interesting point there. I returned to my suite to discover my ship and crew left without me. Left early. And no one told me of it. You want to explain that, Marlon?"

"It's not my fault you get too drunk to answer your comm link," Marlon said defensively. He seemed to forget that he was the senior officer—and twice Kor's age—in light of the marksman's easy air of superiority.

"I think you're projecting," Kor said calmly. "I'm not the one with the drinking problem. Or the communication problem."

"Enough!" Marlon snapped. "I'll not have some marksman questioning my orders or my actions. Find something on board to fix or find somewhere to lie low. I've got my own matters to see to."

Gibson and Kor watched Marlon storm—as best one can storm through a low doorway—off the bridge.

"Man's got a lot on his mind," Gibson said, as if Kor wanted an apology from anyone.

Kor lifted his sopping duffle bag to his shoulder and left the bridge without another word.

That left Gibson with no one to hide his relief from. Or so he believed. Once alone, he flopped into Khiry's chair and swiveled to face her console. The chair squeaked ominously.

He pressed a few buttons to bring up a star chart on the monitor directly before him. He shuddered involuntarily at the thought of the uniformed USPS officer on the communications monitor to the left of it, wondering how long the government would take to trace the ship and come after them.

He punched in some numbers and coordinates and watched the Panger system appear on the screen. With a few more key strokes, he entered a course correction for the planet Pangaea. He pressed "execute." Then he erased the history of his actions. It would be easy enough for someone like Khiry or Jay, the computer tech, to recall this when the time came, but for now it would at least keep prying eyes from noticing they were off course for a few days. And a few days was all Gibson needed.

With a smug smile, Gibson left the bridge unattended.

The stowaway waited a few minutes before she lifted the compartment panel out of her way. She stepped quietly onto the bridge with a leather-soled boot. Sensible, breathy cotton coveralls tucked cleanly into the tops of her boots at mid-calf. Beneath the brown material she sported an athletic frame of toned muscle.

She leaned the panel quietly against the bulkhead and slipped across the floor to Khiry's station. Her smooth movements fitted the grace of a dancer. Despite her mere sixteen years, she'd been in these situations before. Quick, quiet. Her long plaited dreadlocks were tied back in three simple bows to keep them not only neat, but also out of the way. Her smooth caramel skin shimmered in the starlight streaming in from the Instigator's windows; she almost blended into her clothing and surroundings.

She glanced back at the doorway with amber eyes that shifted in color like the walls of the Grand Canyon on Earth, and then turned to her work. With sleek, slender fingers familiar with the work of a spy, she pressed the numbers and coordinates for their current system.

"Pangaea," she whispered with a sly smile. "Not today, my friend. This transport is needed elsewhere. Somewhere much much closer."

She entered a course correction for Eldora Prime and pressed "execute." With the same stealth and speed she'd used to appear, she secreted herself back in the hidden compartment with its small shaft that led through the venting system of the ship. She intended to check out the captain's mystery in the cargo hold.

Chapter Three

Most of the crew had assembled in the mess hall, small as it was, when the fire broke out in the cargo hold. But they couldn't attend to the fire with the ship hitting deceleration and entering a planet's atmosphere unpiloted. Khiry would be hard-pressed later to decide which event was the most surprising. It should have taken at least three days to reach Earth.

To reach Earth: That was the topic of discussion in the yellowish mess hall with its inefficient incandescent light bulb hanging baldly from a cord in the middle of the low ceiling. If not for a three-meter wide slab of table extending most of the length of the room, the bulb would have been broken a dozen times in a shift by people using the doorways on either end of the mess hall as entrance to a thoroughfare. It swung precariously even during their impromptu meeting as if begging someone to stand up suddenly and bang into it, ending its tour of duty.

"Look, you're getting nowhere with questions about cargo," Gibson finally said to Khiry. He had leaned his chair on its back two legs, propping it against the stark metal cabinetry that lined one wall of the short kitchen. Above the cabinetry, it seemed someone had blowtorched out a sensible amount of space for Shayla to cook in. Over that, stubby cabinets reached toward the low ceiling. The room could trigger an onset of claustrophobia in anyone not already affected by the doorways he or she had to stoop to get through. The room could also make a seasoned fighter wonder what was hidden here to warrant so many dents and scratches in the metal panels. Simple kitchen accidents didn't explain these kinds of "wounds" on the walls and cabinets.

"Forget about it," Gibson continued. "Stay out of the hold and let the officials unload whatever it is when we get to Earth. You live in suspense for three days. Big deal. What we need to figure out is how to deal with the officials when we get there."

No one would guess Gibson's smug smile today meant they weren't landing on Earth.

Khiry scowled deeply at the security chief. She had no faith in him or his abilities. It was one of the reasons why she carried a bowie knife in her boot and a plasma gun in a holster at her hip. Always. The weapons she carried belied the sweet-n-simple looks she sported.

"Gibson has a point," Kor muttered, obviously not pleased to agree with the youth. "It doesn't matter what's in the hold now, unless it's going to explode and endanger us all." He turned his deep brown eyes on Marlon. "Is it?"

"Of course not," the captain said, waving his hand as if the suggestion weren't worth considering. "And I resent the implication that I'd put—"

"So what we focus on instead is how to fix the mess the captain put us in when he defied the USPS and took us off Eldora Moon without ACI consent," Jay said. This was the crew's obligatory alien. Originally from the Panger system, he'd learned the common Earth languages of English and Hindi, and could fix up a human or alien computer in the blink of an eye.

Also, he knew to keep himself from mixing. So he'd become not just an asset to Marlon's crew, but also a trusted member of the dysfunctional family over the past couple of years. Of course, he was still an alien, and his idiosyncrasies made him seem slightly *off* to most humans. Crew members usually referred to him as Mozart, implying insanity as well as creativity with computer programs.

Being an alien didn't mean he had any strange protrusions from his forehead or some funky color to his skin. He looked remarkably like a human. There seemed to be a little bit more mass to him; something suggested there were more organs inside that he didn't chat about in casual conversation. Maybe something beneath the extra layer of clothes that always covered his core. Maybe something behind the eyes that sported a pair of baby-blue corrective lenses.

"We *had* ACI consent," Marlon bristled.

"We're not in a mess," Gibson said, defending his captain and uncle. "We just have a misunderstand—"

"Not in a mess?" Khiry exclaimed. "We powered our weapons up against ACI. We cut off their transmission and lifted off against orders to power down. What makes that a *misunderstanding?*"

"We can say we thought they targeted another vessel," Gibson said.

"Oh, please," Khiry said. "Let's make rational suggestions."

"The only person the officer saw was Khiry," Marlon said, as if he formed an idea as he spoke. "We could use her as our scapegoat."

Khiry stared at him in slack-jawed amazement.

Kor frowned. Normally, the lad's soft beard with its surrounding two-day scorch of stubble gave a strong, overly-masculine look to him. It made him look older than his twenty years. When he frowned—seriously frowned in anger—he adopted a severe, fierce look instead. Marlon stopped talking. He probably stopped forming his idea.

Gibson wasn't quite as bright. His Nazi-Germany features lit up, blue eyes shining as if his leader had provided the perfect alibi for genocide—or treason. "You're onto something there. She's safe with us, of course. But we offer her up as our sacrifice. Tell the USPS that she acted out of stupidity. All a mistake. She's too young for the duties we've given her. And we beg for forgiveness for her. We stand up at her trial telling—"

"Gibson," Jay the alien said. "Shut up. No one's using Khiry for their scapegoat without answering to me first."

The security chief didn't get a chance to deride the alien about his origins or *his* usual cockamamie theories because they were interrupted.

"Hey! Looks like a mini party!" Red announced, bouncing into the already tight room. She scraped a metal chair across the metal floor and dropped into it; her ample behind overflowed the seat slightly. She crossed her arms to exaggerate her cleavage and leaned forward on the table, not quite spilling out of her low-cut t-shirt. Her fly-away red hair stopped moving a few seconds after she did as if some invisible wind in the mess hall had followed her. She smacked gum in her oversized mouth and grinned with wide, plump lips.

Khiry noted that the woman's lips had recently seen the collagen injection gun. Red was nothing if not vain. Her long lashes were caked with loads of mascara and her lids tattooed with thick black eyeliner to ensure her fudge-brown eyes stood out from her ruddy complexion.

"What's up with that liftoff, guys? That was rough on my engines."

No one answered immediately. Engaging Red in conversation was like putting wood splinters under your fingernails. Most men kept her around for one purpose. She used to be a tighter. The captain kept her because she could keep the engines in good repair. That and her other purpose.

"We had some trouble with weight," a gentleman named Jack finally told her.

Red fixed him in her lusty stare. Jack's nickname, Idol, made him easy to stare at. It superseded the typical "Doc" that most ship's medics get labeled with. He worked in the ship's sick bay and usually kept to himself. At times like this, he reminded everyone of how kind he was.

Marlon growled.

The diminutive Shayla cleared her throat carefully, lowly, and leaned slightly forward in her chair. "Perhaps," she began. She physically cringed as all eyes turned to her. "Perhaps, when we drop out of hyperdrive, we could send a prepared message to USPS on Earth explaining that we had a miscommunication when we left Eldora Moon. We could take that part of the responsibility. Say that we know there was a problem and we're confused as to what happened."

"Of course you'd say 'confusion,' you melon," Gibson said.

"Shut up," Khiry snapped at him.

"Watch your manners," Jack told Gibson. "Shayla's got a point. If we make the first move, show we're willing to say something went wrong but we don't know what, it'll go a long way toward saving us from getting shot out of the sky before we land."

Kor snickered because the burly wall of muscle rarely laughed outright. "Always good to avoid getting spanged out of the sky."

Another man spoke. This one, Trane, was nicknamed Bay because he had pushed more than one "enemy" out the airlock in his day. "I like Shayla's idea. But we need to add more."

"You're all kidding, right?" Captain Marlon asked in disbelief. "You're suggesting we announce our arrival to USPS and tell them we thumbed our nose at their ACI on Eldora Moon? You're suggesting we do this on the advice of the dumbest melon that's ever set foot on a transport vessel." He pointed a thick and meaty finger in Shayla's direction. "The only thing this tighter's good for is pagging and I doubt any one of you's confirmed *that* yet."

"Here now," yet another crew member interjected. "She keeps this ship dry." Maas spoke of luck with a fairly new Earth expression. She was typically as quiet a lady as Shayla, but bigger, beefier, older, darker of hair and complexion, and far more superstitious. She knew her way around a transport vessel, and while she didn't always make the transports aboard feel comfortable, she at least got them safe and sound to their destinations. No space-sickness. No lift-off whiplash. That sort of thing.

In this conversation, her concern was getting the captain to stop demeaning Shayla. The fairy-looking little lady was, as far as Maas was concerned, something of a good-luck charm on board.

Stoic little Shayla leaned back in her chair quietly while the personalities at the table erupted in defense of her honor and her plan or in defense of *sneaking* the ship and its mysterious cargo onto Earth instead. The yelling and pounding of fists on the table made her start from time to time.

Finally, Jack the medic leaned over to Shayla and said quietly, so only she could hear, "I've had all of this I can stand. I'm going to check out what's in the hold."

Her eyes went wide in alarm. "You can't! Idol, it sounds dangerous. If Marlon doesn't fire you out the airlock, whatever's in there could harm you."

"What did you call me?"

She blinked, confused by his question. As she realized she'd called him by his descriptive nickname, she blushed.

He winked at her. "No worries, Pet. Look, I intend to figure out what's up his bum," he jerked his head toward Marlon to indicate the captain. "I'll report back. Your plan's a good one. Don't let them tell you otherwise."

She smiled at his kindness as he got up to leave.

No one noticed his departure. To argue was too much a part of their dynamic, and this argument was worth continuing. They'd gotten around to what they wanted to put in a message beyond "we were confused" if they opted to go in and announce their arrival to the United Society for Peace and Strength on Earth. Gibson, who thought the argument moot, went right along with the announcement idea.

Ten or so minutes later, the fire alarm sounded.

Unfortunately, that's when the ship lurched and a proximity alarm sounded.

"Smear it all, we're headed into atmosphere!" Khiry shouted.

* * * * *

The stowaway appreciated not just Jack's chivalry, but also his handsome features. She couldn't guess that he was a doctor. She just liked the strong look of him. He was the sort you recruit to your cause—the sort you get to help your older brother beat back the resistance on Earth.

She slipped through the ship's vents unnoticed as he made his way to the cargo hold. She'd already looked inside. She'd already seen the monsters Captain Marlon had brought on board. She already knew what he carried to Earth to aid the resistance against the United Society for Peace and Strength.

As Jack stepped into the spacious cargo hold, he let his eyes adjust to the darkness. The hall he'd come from wasn't well-lit by any stretch of the imagination, but this giant room of barrels, metal shipping containers, wooden boxes, and steel cages was lit by simple LED sconces spaced every few meters along the perimeter. The steel balcony above with its mesh floor seemed to have more frequent lights but the placement of the transports' luggage blocked most of it from reaching the doorway he'd opened. For some reason, he felt the need to leave the door open. Its heavy metal bulk spoke of some sort of finality whenever closed. He didn't want that finality shut behind him.

In her mind, the stowaway thanked the stars that Jack left the door open. She willed him to turn around and exit through it.

Instead, Jack pulled a flashlight from his belt and switched it on. Its crisp bluish light fell in a larger pool from the conical beam he pointed toward the floor. He used this to cut a winding path through the boxes and crates toward the back of the hold. He knew the captain wouldn't hide something important right at the front. Nothing that the United Society for Peace and Strength would be after would be easy to spot.

He moved toward a towering mass of black and reddish bulges consuming the back half of the hold. To Jack's surprise, these bulges moved slowly, carefully, taking up the space beneath the balcony. More to his surprise, these bulges were obviously behind heavy vertical bars.

"What the devil?" he muttered.

As Jack moved closer, he lifted the beam of his light up toward the towering masses. He didn't have a lot of time to take in the details of the creatures he saw. He certainly didn't have time to cry out for help. One of the beasts pulled back its head, opened its mouth, and shot forth a stream of flame.

Chapter Four

The stowaway screamed, but no one heard her over the roar of the dragon and its fire. No one heard her over the ship's proximity alarm in its buzzing frenzy. No one heard her over Jack's scream of terror, and then pain, as a dragon's gaseous fire caught his clothes, hair, and skin, and began consuming him from the outside in. He spun to get away, dropped the flashlight as if it were the culprit, and banged into a wooden crate. Ricocheting from that crate to something tied up in cloths to a lidless barrel that tipped under his weight, Jack stumbled like Frankenstein's monster, spreading the fire in a crazed path of destruction.

The stowaway jumped from her hiding place to grab an extinguisher. She knew it was too late to save the quieting man, but the cargo hold was going up in flames. She had to get the fire under control or the ship was in danger. *I have to get to Eldora Prime,* she thought.

The dragons watched her and backed from the bars of their cage. They moaned and grumbled in their dragon fear of the chaos and noise erupting in the ship.

* * * * *

Khiry beat everyone to the bridge and landed in her chair to its familiar squeak beneath the buzz of the ship's alarm. Red called on the communication system, "I've pulled the fuel out of the reaction. You've got ion."

With a grimace, Khiry flipped switches and slammed buttons, changing the propulsion from chemical reaction to mere ion to slow and control the descent. She wasn't sure they had time.

"Where the hell are we?" Marlon demanded, puffing up the two steps to his bridge's doorway.

Kor had beat him by several paces and was already at his station, powering up for a fight. "You want me to fire at the surface?"

"What?" Marlon asked, obviously confused.

"It may come to that," Khiry said.

"What?" Marlon asked again.

Gibson had stumbled in by then and said, "To slow our drop."

"Won't make that much difference," Marlon snarled.

"At this rate, every little bit will help," Khiry said through clenched teeth. "We're in trouble." She lifted one hand from her constant barrage on the console keys to pull the communication device from its cradle above her and pushed the button on its side. "All hands. Find a seat and strap yourself in if possible. We're about to experience a hard landing."

She released the device; it hung dangling, swinging to and fro beside her, as she went back to punching at the keys. "We're still at Eldora," she announced in surprise. "We've been traveling at that speed for nearly an hour right toward Eldora Prime."

Gibson frowned.

Marlon slammed his palm against the handle above him. "What the devil did you do, Khiry? I'll have Trane fire you out the airlock if you've got us all killed!"

She muttered some curses about his manhood while she worked at the controls. "We'll see landscape in a minute. You ready over there, Kor?"

"Ready."

She could hear the whine of plasma canons and the whir of photon streamers set at maximum. He would hit it with all he had. God help anyone living near their "landing" site.

"I'll steer clear of any terraformers," she said. She figured no one was listening to that, but Kor responded.

"That's the best plan I've heard since the mess hall."

She couldn't hide a little smile. Marlon groused some sort of curse.

Then they saw it. Land. Out of the clouds, mountains peeked at them like shards of jagged death.

"Aw, smear it all. Mountains," she said.

"Another good thing to steer clear of," Kor muttered.

Marlon gripped the handle above him tighter and Gibson fled the bridge.

"Sending you map and trajectory," Jay's voice called through the communication system. Just like that, a topographical map appeared on Khiry's screen directly before her.

"I love you, Mozart!" Khiry called, as if he could have heard her wherever he was in the ship without the flip of any switches. It was as if the alien had read her mind. *He knows me like a computer manual,* she thought, but spared no further thoughts for him. They were crashing. She glanced from the window to the screen, from the screen to the window, nudging the ship to the south and west of the mountain range.

"A peggin' ocean!" she announced next.

"We can't survive this," Kor muttered.

"Is that a city?" Marlon asked.

"Civilization. Want to miss them but get help later," Kor said.

"Thought you said we weren't surviving this?" Khiry mocked.

"That's before I saw civilization," he teased right back.

"Hittin' the brakes," she called out. "This is it." She maneuvered the ship into the equivalent of some kind of mid-air skid. "Give us some joy, Kor!"

He hit the photon streamers and everyone felt the jerk.

Down in the cargo hold, the dragons tousled against one another. Flaming crates banged against their cage, startling howls and roars from them. The stowaway was long gone.

On the bridge, Khiry let out a gasp. "I can't control it. We're gonna hit."

Kor fired another blast of weapons, pointing them directly at the ground.

"We can't coast!" she yelled.

"I'm digging us a landing strip."

"It won't matter—"

Their strategy stopped abruptly as the Instigator hit the surface of Eldora Prime.

Chapter Five

She wasn't sure how long she'd been out. It couldn't have been too long because the ship was still on fire when she felt pain. Something in the back of her mind—probably a migraine or a concussion—told her to wake up. And fast.

Khiry opened her eyes to the sound of someone's moans. It was a girl's voice. Not her own.

"Shayla?" she mumbled, tasting the copper sting of blood in her mouth. She spit a cheek full of blood and saliva over the side of her console, suddenly aware that the dim light of a planet's dusk spilled easily around her, comforting her like a cloak. A breeze full of saltwater and floral scents wafted over her, bringing a coolness that promised to worsen as darkness deepened.

The smell of charred metal and melted electronics mixed with the planet's flowers when the breeze stilled. Obviously the wind came from the south and the majority of the ship was behind her, to the north. She wondered how far south she'd coasted from the mountains.

She pushed herself up off the crumpled console to a sitting position, assessing herself all the while. Apart from aches and pains, particularly the pain in her head, it didn't seem like anything was broken. She picked up her left hand to glare at a deep gash that bled profusely. *That's not so dry,* she thought.

The rush of wind over tall grasses sent a chill through her, reminding her that night would fall here soon. A quick look around proved the bridge of the Instigator had been utterly destroyed in the crash. Her survival was a miracle. No doubt Captain Marlon, standing like a pompous fool at impact, had been flung from the wreckage and now existed in several broken, lifeless pieces.

As helmswoman, she wasn't really next in command, but as more intelligent and better liked than Gibson, she'd likely be appointed the leader of the rag-tag crew left without a captain. She wondered if her age would matter to them. She'd best get busy and assess more than her own wounds. She'd best figure out who among the voices behind her was whole enough to make a shelter out of the wounded ship for the fast-approaching night.

The girl's voice moaned again, drawing Khiry's attention toward the area where the bridge's doorway used to be. She scanned the strewn metal and tufts of grass and dirt to see a brown lady draped across a computer monitor. Her first thought was that they'd landed on one of Eldora Prime's terraformers. As *Wizard of Ozzian* as that theory seemed, she doubted its validity. She knew this wasn't one of the transports. Could she be a stowaway? *Bad karma for her,* Khiry thought.

She struggled onto her hands and knees, ignoring the trail of blood her hand left as she made her way the few meters to the lady. "Do you think you've broken anything?" she asked.

The girl's eyes opened to reveal a lovely amber color as deep as veins of the gem in a mine shaft. Khiry sat back in surprise. Something seemed familiar about this beautiful young woman and it was something noble like royalty.

"Nothing feels broken."

"Who are you?" Khiry asked.

The girl smiled faintly, her rich brown lips curving seductively. "Electra."

Between the familiar face and the first name, Khiry didn't need a family name to make any more connections. This was Electra Endh, sister to Earth's USPS leader, Presidente Lamahl Endh. Of the few dozen questions that shot through Khiry's pounding brain, the one that made it to her tongue astonished them both, "Can you influence the people on this planet to help us?"

Electra's smile deepened. "Khiry Okerson. A leader after all. I think we're going to need that. This planet's new colony has been silent for too many moons."

Khiry frowned. "What?"

Electra slipped quietly into unconsciousness, leaving Khiry to figure that one out while she looked around for crew members. She looked first in the direction of the marksman's station.

"Kor?" she called.

The man mumbled some sort of response from beneath twisted metal and wires. "This is not so dry," she muttered sarcastically. "Am I the only one unharmed up here?"

The sting of her wounded hand reminded her that she wasn't unharmed. She'd have to find a bandage of some sort for herself. She hoped Jack was among the voices calling out to each other in the wreckage; he could swab the hand with some kind of disinfectant and get her patched up in no time.

She moved with better ease to Kor's side and lifted a panel from his legs. His console was nowhere to be seen. A mass of wires and cables had wrapped around his upper torso, essentially securing him to the bulkhead at his side. If not for those wires, she had no doubt he'd have been carried away in the mess of windows and front end of the ship now missing from their wreckage.

"You look no worse for wear," she said, trying to minimize the welts and bruises on his arms.

He snorted. "Trying to be positive, are you? Help me get out of this tangled mess, O optimistic one. Where's Marlon?"

"If we're lucky, he's dead."

Kor snorted again. "Did I hear you talking to Shayla?"

She avoided his eyes as she pulled her bowie knife from her boot. "No. There's a stowaway here." She wondered if she should tell him who the girl was. Of course, Kor was a smart guy. He'd take one look at Electra and guess who she was. There was no hiding her identity. "It's Electra Endh."

"*The* Electra Endh?"

"One and only." Khiry began cutting at the cables to free him. "She's passed out right now."

"Is she the cargo Marlon was hiding?"

"Maybe part of it. I know there's something down there too heavy for this ship's engines. Something that's burning at the moment. I'd like to get you up and help the crew get that fire out. It's down, I can tell from here, but God only knows what happens to us if the cargo blows."

He nodded, helping her untangle the rest of the wires. "Extinguishers?"

"Probably all over the place. I can hear spraying back there," she jerked her head toward the back of the mangled mass of ship. *That hurt,* she thought. "Sounds like extinguishers," she said aloud.

"Other survivors?"

"I imagine so. The rest of the crew would know to get in there and get the fire out."

He frowned. "What else do I hear?"

She didn't understand his question. The only sound, other than the dying of a fire and the groan of the ship as it settled in this new gravity in its new contortions, was that of people finding each other. They called out words of encouragement, words of instruction. Someone hollered at crew member Maas to sit off to the side to rest—obviously Maas was injured.

"Khiry!" Jay called. He headed toward the bridge section to check on her.

It was good to see their smartest crew member alive.

"I hear something heavy," Kor said.

"Heavy?" she asked, obviously doubting his level of consciousness or ability to reason fully in his injured state. How could something *sound* heavy? That's when she heard it, too. Something with incredible mass lumbered toward their crash site.

Someone who fought the dwindling fire behind them screamed.

Chapter Six

The scream served several purposes. It woke Electra again, stirring her into sluggish but certain motion. She was up on her hands and knees when Kor reached down to scoop her up in one burly arm. His other arm carried what appeared to be a rapid-fire plasma streamer canon, but the gun had obviously been modified somehow. It seemed bulkier than a normal plasma streamer weapon. Khiry would wonder later how he'd kept it attached to himself during the crash.

The scream also sent the crew members in the back of the ship into new action. From their various positions, they grabbed up weapons or ducked into hidden compartments now strengthened by crossed beams or bent trusses. Maas had jumped from her resting place on a grassy rock outside the ship's protective shell, but she jumped too late.

Khiry's steps stuttered as she moved through the ship, stopping her beside a torn opening in the bulkhead, and she stared at Maas being lifted into the dusky air. Something had seized the screaming woman. Something solid and hulking, but not much taller than an oversized man. Was this the heavy presence she and Kor had heard? *How could something merely the size of a big guy have that much mass? How could it possibly…*

She stopped her musing when the bi-ped creature tilted back its head and opened its maw, the jaws unhinged like an armed, upright python. A round row of jagged incisors protruded from the enlarged mouth, reaching for Maas as if the mouth was its own entity, separate from the creature and starving.

Maas screamed a frenetic series of high-pitched shrieks in the short time left to her. It took only seconds for the creature to puncture her mid-section, to tear through clothing and flesh and bone, to feast on organs and tissue while her blood rose up to choke the screams to a gurgling, blessed stop.

Blessed for the petrified crew listening.

Khiry tore her gaze from the scene to move on, to follow Kor, but he had stopped and was watching her. His eyes sought hers for just a moment. In that moment, the crewmates shared a wealth of emotions and information. What he would have asked, she answered in her wide brown stare of stark horror. *Keep moving. Get to the group*, it seemed to say. He obeyed the unspoken command without question.

"Kor!" Shayla yelled. Her innocent voice echoed off the walls, ceiling, and floor around them as if it were broadcasting on some old Belgium radio station on Earth. A steel-like sound reverberated to the heavens. She stood at a juncture in the Instigator's dark halls, a ghost of sorts among the haunting emergency lights glowing against all odds every ten meters.

He put a finger to his lips, nearly scraping the enormous gun against the bent and folded metal ceiling panels above them. The small red-haired woman glanced to Electra hanging limply over his other arm, but obeyed Kor's signal. She said nothing more.

Jay had already reached the group and grabbed Electra from Kor. He helped the woman run alongside him as he spoke quietly to Khiry, "We're getting back to the cargo hold. It's the safest place to make a stand."

Electra's eyes went wide. "No!"

Ah, Khiry thought. *Now we find out what's down there. Now when it's too late to do anything about it.*

* * * * *

Luckily, most of the crew not only survived the crash, but survived the attack of the man-like beasts with their terrible mouths. Trane, better known as Bay for his murderous ways; Jay, the intelligent alien; Gibson, the security chief who carried more weapons than it seemed his wiry frame could support; Kor, the muscular and capable marksman; Shayla, the stealthy but simple chef; Red, the openly aggressive engineer; Khiry, the type A personality whose ship had just crashed on a foreign world; Electra, the United Society for Peace and Strength leader's beautiful sister; and four of the seven transports who'd paid for passage to Earth sought shelter in the cargo hold with five dragons.

Khiry stood a few feet from the bent and angled bars of the cage staring in wonder. She'd heard that there were dragons on Eldora Moon, but hadn't seen them in all the weeks she'd spent there. Now she came face to face with four of them. Well, five if you counted the one that looked wounded, laying on its back as if using its wings for a makeshift hospital bed.

She was awestruck.

"Could use your help, Khiry!" Kor shouted.

She had suggested they stack crates against the doorway for the night to keep the man-beasts out. They all hoped against hope that morning would take the demonesque creatures back to whatever lair they slept in and give the Instigator's crew some reprieve. In the meantime, something had to be done against the creatures' incredible strength and maddening drive.

As if in denial of all sources of danger, Khiry stood in silence, marveling at the dragons before her. Their scent of limestone and dirt mixed with the scent of human fear and sweat in the confines of the cargo hold. The remnants of fire and smoke masked any other smells the space may have held.

She first examined their barrier, noting that it had been damaged in the crash, but had held better than even the hull of the Instigator. These creatures obviously had the kind of strength that the man-beasts out on the planet did. Or more. And someone—she was betting Marlon—had sought to keep that strength behind heavy bars.

She coughed some of the hold's smoke out of her lungs. Jay tossed a glance her way to make sure she was all right. He was no doctor, but could perform basic triage. They already knew what had happened to their doctor thanks to Electra's quick and concise tale of it; Jay would fill in as best he could.

Despite what the beasts had done to Jack, Khiry turned her attention to the dragons without any real fear of them. They were exquisite. Of course she'd read fantasy books on the United Society for Peace and Strength's bibliotheca. What else was there to do on those long journeys through short space? She'd read *Beowulf*. She'd read *The Hobbit*. She'd read *Choices Meant for Kings*. She knew what the great fantasy authors thought these beasts looked and acted like. Now she had them to study for real.

One dragon in particular seemed willing to be studied— or to study her. The darkest of the four still standing had moved slowly toward her, shifting his massive bulk on strong front legs and stronger hind legs. His head was as long as Kor's torso, but not quite as wide. It sloped from a rounded black nose with sensitive-looking scales back to a wider jaw hinge. At the top of his head, two black anterior horns appeared to almost wave in their shape back to two sharp points.

He held his massive wings so close against his body that she couldn't see just how big or wide they truly were. As they lay folded like enormous black silk sails with bones for accordion flexing, their tips towered a good two meters above his head with hand-like claws at the very top. Even the nails of these claws were black as obsidian. And as shiny. The creature's long, thick neck rose out of the muscled, bulky body like a black marble statue. It was graceful. Each black scale shone as if etched by a sculptor's perfect hand specifically to catch light in dimly lit places and reflect it like onyx.

"Onyx," she breathed.

The creature blinked gray-blue eyes as if listening for another word. He seemed pleased with the way she spoke this one.

"You're beautiful like the onyx stone made from Chalcedony on Earth," she said quietly. "Men carve it into vases and cameos that sell for thousands of dollars. Even in this economic time, people fight for items of beauty made of jade and amethyst and onyx. If people of Earth could see you, they would probably worship you."

The dragon lowered its massive head so its eyes were level with hers. Its huge mouth full of teeth that lined the jaws like a crocodile's opened slightly. Would he speak? Dragons of Eldora Moon couldn't possibly know the common languages of Earth. Instead, the creature made a gurgling sound, almost as if he gargled some word in his throat. He sounded pleased.

Khiry smiled at him. "May I touch you?" she asked tentatively.

The dragon tilted his large head slightly, watching her mouth move. As if the loud calls from crew members and banging of super-strong beasts outside the cargo hold door were part of another world, Khiry and the dragon stared at each other in wonder. They had discovered something new. Not all humans were bad. Not all dragons were bad.

She extended her hand slowly through the hanging haze, showing him her palm. With care, she let her hand pass the bars of the cage. She stopped short of touching the wild, unknown beast, leaving her hand mere centimeters from him, palm still face-up. The dragon closed the gap, leaning his rough and scaly chin into the warmth of her touch.

Her smile broadened as she watched his gray-blue eyes brighten.

She had to get him out of the cage before the man-beasts got into the cargo hold.

Chapter Seven

"You can't be serious," Gibson stuttered.

"If those creatures get in here and get that cage open, they'll have the dragons cornered. The dragons won't stand a chance," Khiry argued.

"And what part of that is our problem?" Gibson asked.

Khiry stamped her foot in frustration.

"Khiry's right," Shayla said. "We have to give them a fighting chance."

"Oh, the melon has decreed it," Gibson mocked. "I guess we have to do it, now."

Kor snatched the plasma gun from his belt and cocked it as he put it to Gibson's throat. It whined with power. "I disabled the stun setting on this weapon ages ago. Now apologize to the lady."

Gibson snarled as he muttered something that sounded remarkably like "sorry."

"Now, let's discuss this nicely. Shayla, Khiry *does* have a good point. It's not the dragons' fault that they're here. It's Marlon's fault. We can do right by letting them out to have a fighting chance. But how safe do we feel turning five dragons loose among us?"

"I don't think they mean us harm," Khiry said.

"You didn't see them cook your doctor," Electra said. "You have seen a soft and gentle side of these wild beasts so far, but I have seen something else in them. They meant your man harm. I was hiding in the panels when it happened. He never had the chance you're wanting to give these beasts. You must be careful what you give freedom to. The Free can turn on those who grant liberty in hope of taking more than their fare share."

"Your brother's politics aren't welcome here," Jay sniped.

"And what's it to you? Aren't you an alien?" one of the transports asked.

Khiry frowned at the man who had spoken. "Here now. We're getting off topic. Alien or not, Mozart saved your hide when we were avoiding the mountains out there." Despite the pain still throbbing in the back of her head, Khiry nodded in Jay's direction so the transport couldn't mistake who she referred to. "Now he's part of the crew that's going to save your hide again. Who's to say these dragons aren't also part of the crew that'll save us from these beasts? The enemy of my enemy is my friend."

Up to this point, Red had been uncharacteristically quiet. The idea of dragons on board the ship frightened her, of course, but seeing Khiry befriend one of them loosened her up a bit. She slowly approached the dragons' cage out of curiosity while the debate carried on behind her. Gibson seemed to be the only one out of sorts over it. Even Electra, who had seen Jack die, sounded as if she could be persuaded to Khiry's point of view. Interesting. Red wondered what about these creatures so appealed to Khiry that she'd fight to release them into their midst.

"Apart from Khiry's use of Arabian proverbs, what do we have to convince us these dragons would help us?" Kor asked. "As far as they know, we caged them and brought them to some foreign planet. Now evil beasts that look something like us on this foreign planet are going to try to kill them."

Jay looked to the transport nearest him. "I'm sorry. I don't know what an Arabian proverb is."

The female transport shrugged. It was obvious she felt uncomfortable now that she knew she sat next to an alien. "Something before my time on Earth."

Red tried to tune out the conversation. She was too intrigued by the mythical creatures before her to let the crews' words distract her. The large, reddish-black dragon currently stared at her. The other three uninjured dragons huddled around the wounded one. *Like elephants,* Red thought. It was well known that the elephants of Earth had worried over injured companions and fondled their dead, unwilling to leave fallen comrades. She wondered if that's why they went extinct—elephants starving to death keeping watch over elephant graveyards. Not everything could be attributed to global warming and shifting climate zones. She also wondered if the wounded dragon was going to die. It seemed a shame to lose such a pretty creature. Just like it was a shame when the last elephant died on Earth.

As if it took great effort, the reddish-black dragon shifted its weight to move toward her. Obviously it was difficult to move in the cramped space with four dragons to maneuver around, but she made it over to the bars and stared out at Red as if expecting something to happen. Red stared back. *If Khiry can pet a dragon, I should be able to as well,* Red thought. She smiled up at the creature and reached, slowly, as Khiry had done, toward the bars. She let her hand carefully pass the bars, palm up, and stop a few centimeters from the dragon's lovely reddish-black snout.

The dragon blinked her reddish-brown eyes. She seemed rather sad for a dragon about to make her first contact with a human. Her contact surprised everyone.

In a sudden flash of reddish scales and yellowed teeth, the dragon snapped. As fast as a snapping turtle takes the end off a stick, the dragon clamped down on Red's wrist, biting cleanly through flesh, sinew, and bone. Red screamed as the dragon spit out the twitching hand. No one could tell which won the race to the floor—hand or woman.

Khiry reached Red's crumpled form first. She gathered the pale woman's upper body into her lap, grabbing up the affected limb, and calling out for a rag, a cloth, a strip of anything to tie off the bleeding club. "Her radial artery's pumping hard. Kor, we need to cauterize—"

"Got it," he said, already powering up the gun in his hand. "Khiry, I don't know if this thing can do it without damaging her more."

"Do we have another?"

"I have one," a transport said. "Its stun setting still works." The man gave Kor a meaningful glance as he handed over the weapon.

"Thank you," Jay supplied.

The two performing triage weren't acknowledging anything at the moment.

The dragons obviously argued among themselves. From guttural barkings to slappings with wings, the onyx dragon and a lesser black one appeared to be chastising the reddish-black one for her attack on Red.

"Hold her tight," Kor said. "This'll probably wake her."

Shayla cringed and turned away. Trane had stepped close to watch the operation and put a protective arm around the small woman.

The sound of the gun's whine reached everyone before the stench of burning flesh did. One of the transports fainted. The dragons' arguing reached a climax and the reddish-black one fell to the metal floor with a great rumbling of the cargo hold.

Red awoke with a start as the pain of cauterization seared through meaty tissue, but Kor had nearly finished the operation by then. Khiry tightened her hold on the woman as she came to screaming for help. The cries turned to sobbing profanities as Shayla rushed over to dab her forehead with a cloth. Khiry figured out that it was the sleeve of Shayla's shirt.

"There now," Shayla cooed. "They've saved your life. Calm and relax, calm and relax."

"She's in shock," Gibson said.

"Can someone help her over…over somewhere…" Khiry stammered.

Two of the transports who had not fainted rushed in then to lift the pale woman and carry her to another section of the hold. They could be heard consoling her and praying over her. Red continued sobbing pitifully.

"You see what they're capable of?" Electra said. There was no triumph in her voice; it was a statement of fact.

"I don't understand," Khiry mused, still kneeling against the metal floor where Red's blood crept toward her legs.

"She must have done something," Shayla said in her childlike voice. "I can't imagine one of these beautiful creatures just attacking for no reason."

"You can't imagine?" Electra said. "They attacked Jack for no reason. Jack. Your friend."

"No, look," Khiry said, climbing to her feet.

All eyes turned to follow her extended arm, to follow her finger pointed toward the dragons' cage where the onyx one held the reddish-black dragon down with one massive back leg. With one front claw, he held up the injured dragon's front leg. It was missing its claw. Just like Red's arm now missed its hand. But the injured dragon's front leg continued to bleed.

Khiry looked to Kor. "Give me your radiator."

"No, you can't possibly—"

"Don't you see? It's the only way they could communicate to us."

"They could've showed us that before," Gibson said. "They didn't have to maim a girl to tell us one of their own was missing a hand."

"They wanted to see what to do," Khiry said, almost begging to be believed. "Now they know how we'll fix it."

"You're really stretching there," a transport said.

"You can't get in there to help that dragon without compromising the integrity of the whole cage. They'll all easily get out," Electra said.

"Then our debate is finished," Khiry said.

"And what if one of them decides a hand is not enough?" Electra asked. "What if one of them's hungry?"

"I'll take full responsibility," Khiry said.

"Responsibility?" Electra and Gibson guffawed in unison. The two could wonder at their unlikely symphony later. Electra finished the thought: "No one will care about personal responsibility once bodies start piling up. Dead is dead."

"Then you can go out with those man-beasts and make friends among them. I'm taking my chances with the dragons." Khiry grabbed the radiator gun from Kor's grip before he had any further objections and marched over to the dragon cage.

"Is no one going to stop this insanity?" a female transport asked. "I don't want to end up eaten by a dragon."

No one responded and the worried woman went to hide behind some crates at the front of the cargo hold.

Khiry motioned for the dragons to back up, as if they had anywhere to go, and pointed the weapon at an angle at one of the bars. It was slow-going, but she got through four bars with it before its power started to wane. She wrenched at the bars with her arms, pulling them loose at the weak points she'd burned. Kor came to help her. No one realized he had moved just an instant before Jay had the chance.

"I don't want to use up the power in my gun, too," Kor said quietly. "We may need it against…" He looked uneasily at the onyx dragon watching them. "Against whatever. Can we get in with just these four bars out?"

"I can. What's this *we* business?" she asked.

"I don't like the idea of sending you in alone."

"I think the onyx one likes me," she said.

"I think you're troubled in the head. You'll need someone to cauterize the wound while you hold the beast." He thought about the dragon's mass. "Or vice versa."

"We may need several people to hold the dragon down, but I don't think anyone else is going to volunteer."

"I'll help," Shayla said.

Neither of them had heard the silent young lady creep up behind them so her announcement startled them. "Shayla, I don't know how you do that," Khiry muttered.

"You think the dragon likes you, too?" Kor asked.

Shayla only smiled her childlike, innocent smile. "He likes me well enough if I'm with Khiry."

Neither of them questioned her strange idea. "Here we go, then," Khiry said, stepping into the cage.

Chapter Eight

It took Kor and Khiry less than a minute to figure out the injured dragon was kin to the reddish-black dragon. Maybe she was an offspring. They were about the same size, but their colorings and markings were identical as far as the two could tell.

"There's nothing dry about this," Gibson muttered, pacing uneasily among the crates. "Nothing dry at all."

While Shayla cooed and said soothing words to the injured dragon, she stroked her head and jaw as if she couldn't snap Shayla's hand off as easily as her friend/mate had just done to Red. Kor and Khiry exchanged a look of discomfort over the creature's massive belly. If they couldn't stop the bleeding, if they were too late, how would the reddish-brown one react? Like T-Rex of the ancient Earth protecting her young, would the reddish-brown one assume they were the culprits and kill them?

Kor looked to Shayla. "Can you hug its head on your lap? Not tight, but firmly? Try to keep it from snapping at us once we start?"

Trane hung on the bars of the cage, waggling one leg in nervous anticipation.

Shayla nodded at Kor, still cooing calmly as she cradled the dragon's head. The dragon rolled her reddish-brown eyes wildly, obviously in pain and fear. It had learned that humans were bad. Here were three surrounding it. With a weapon. Her eyes found the young dragon in the shadows and she made a sound of comfort for its benefit.

The onyx dragon made some sort of guttural sound at them, almost as soothing as Shayla's voice.

"Come around here," Kor instructed Khiry. "I'll hold the arm."

He cocked the weapon and its whine seemed to fill the entire ship. Everyone out in the rest of the cargo hold strained to watch from his or her hiding spot. They barely breathed.

While Kor got into position and handed off the weapon, Khiry reached out to touch Onyx slowly and gently. "This will be terrible at first. I'm so sorry."

She truly felt sorry. She didn't know how to make them understand that she was about to cause awful pain for their injured friend, but the pain would go away. It might save their friend's life. She felt tears well up in her eyes at either her frustration or the dragon's plight. She wasn't sure which.

Onyx still held the reddish-black dragon down on the metal floor, but it was apparent T-Rex was no longer a threat. The lesser black one watched from behind Onyx, obviously wary of the weapon whining in their cage. The fourth uninjured dragon, smaller than the adults, hunkered as far back in the shadow as he could. His color seemed as reddish-black as the injured one. *Junior,* Khiry thought. *God, don't let this injured one be his mother.*

The process was as she expected. Terrible. The dragon howled its pitiful roar. Her flinch wasn't an attempt to get away or to harm the humans, but it was strong enough to lift Kor off the floor. It took Khiry several attempts to get the wound cauterized properly, to be sure it wouldn't start bleeding again. All the while, Shayla offered soft words and even sang a lilting Irish lullaby from Earth to the creature.

When the whole ordeal was complete, Onyx let T-Rex up. She popped up as if the space in the cage had never been a problem for her massive bulk and nearly knocked Kor and Shayla to the floor scooping up her winged friend in what could only be described as a hug. It was a true show of affection. The smaller dragon rushed from out of the shadows to fling himself into this reunion. It was obvious he believed the injured dragon was now saved.

Kor and Shayla joined Khiry on the other side of the opening in the cage bars. "What do you think?" Kor asked.

"I don't know. She lost a lot of blood. Look at this floor."

"I agree," he sighed. "I have no idea how much blood a dragon can lose and survive."

"She was so weak," Shayla murmured.

"What do you mean?" Kor asked. "She nearly threw us into the wall."

"No…she could have done so much more if she was strong. The poor dear."

Kor and Khiry exchanged a worried glance. Again, Khiry wondered what T-Rex would do if this injured one died.

"We should work on getting this cage open or the bars down or something," Kor muttered, as if to himself. He was examining the vertical bars that had been bent and somewhat mangled during the crash. Onyx watched his gaze. When their eyes met, brown pools of worry connecting with gray-blue depths of wisdom, Onyx motioned for them to move.

Khiry decided then and there that when a dragon motions for you to move, you don't hesitate. The three stepped off to the side and watched as Onyx settled himself. He tossed his head as if summoning courage or strength or whatever dragons summon for a task, and then leaned forward and opened his mouth slightly. He blew a slow, careful, steady stream of blue fire at the bars, focusing the blast in a general area away from cargo and flammable boxes on the other side. After a few minutes of this, he sat back and reached forward with one front leg.

One powerful claw wrapped around five bars and squeezed them easily, bending them in on each other. He wrenched them inward and snapped them down.

"Umm. That kind of solves your debate," one of the transports said.

"He's burning up all the oxygen in the hold," Gibson said. "Make him stop."

Onyx had already begun the operation on the next set of bars.

"I don't know how to explain oxygen," Khiry called to Gibson.

"Show him you gasping for air and dying on the ground. He'll get the real picture soon enough if he keeps that up."

"No, I don't think so. It's very quick. I think he'll have all the bars snapped that he needs snapped—"

Jay interrupted her. "We could open the door. It's been a while since we heard anything banging out there."

"So we have man-beasts at the front and dragons at our back?" a transport asked. "No, thank you."

"You'd rather die of asphyxiation?" someone asked her.

"Just get him to stop."

"He'll be done by the time you all are done arguing about it," Kor said. "Just let him finish. If anyone starts to feel light-headed, you're welcome to leave."

A few grumbles followed that statement but they were silenced by a dragon's wail. It was a pitiful sound that subsided into something low and howling. All eyes turned to T-Rex holding her friend so that the smaller dragon could stroke its muzzle. The sounds of distress came from the smaller one; sad little yelps like puppies looking for their mother in a winter storm. The little creature looked up at T-Rex with soulful eyes. Had his eyes been that large before, when he hung back in the shadows watching the humans try to save the adult? The poor thing nuzzled its snout against the dying elder, releasing a torrent of little cries unlike anything the humans had ever heard before. Onyx bowed his head and waited for the little dragon to stop shaking from the onset of sadness.

Khiry wanted to go to the young dragon. She wanted to wrap her arms around him and pet him and offer him the sweet, soft words that Shayla had offered his elder. Her feet refused to move, of course. There was no way she could intrude on this precious moment. Instead, she sat down on the nearest crate to cry.

Chapter Nine

In the still of early morning, Kor shook her gently. Onyx sat like one of the now-buried sphinxes from Egypt next to her, as if guarding her. Yet he had let Kor approach. Apparently Kor was one of the few humans of whom Onyx approved.

"I've gone 'round the perimeter and all looks clear," he whispered. "I think we should get everyone up and move out."

"It's light?"

"Finally. I think the days are short on Eldora Prime," he muttered unhappily.

"I don't know much about it. Electra can help us there."

Kor nodded at the wisdom in her statement. "I've got tents and rations packed for easy carrying. If you don't get offended, I'll suggest the men carry that."

She smiled at him wanly. "If you don't get offended, I'll suggest we take turns relieving ourselves before we get started. I'm about to burst."

He shook his head. "I don't think anyone should do anything alone. Take the other women with you. Groups for everything. And everyone armed to the teeth. There's no evidence those beasts are out there, but we don't know for sure."

She nodded, climbing to her feet. Onyx got up on his haunches.

"It makes sense that light would hurt their eyes. What I saw was something with big, wide orbs. But I like the idea of erring on the side of caution."

"What are you two whispering about?" a transport asked.

"Ah, good," Khiry said. "One less to wake. We're thinking of ways to keep us alive."

* * *

After an argument about using the dragons as packhorses, the group of seven crew members, Electra, and four transports thought they were on their way toward the mountain range. More specifically, they thought they were on their way toward the pre-fabricated city the terraformers had brought and erected just west of the mountain range. While Khiry mentally applauded their choice of building where snowmelt could bring fresh water and a fertile valley could provide good crops, she couldn't help wondering if the foothills of the mountains brought the terrifying man-beasts. She hoped the terraformers had a network for protecting the city and its inhabitants against them.

Electra looked doubtful. She pouted her pretty lips.

"What's wrong?" a transport asked.

"We've not heard from the colonists on Eldora Prime for several moons. It's why I was coming here. To check on them. If the beasts of this planet—"

"Wait a minute," Gibson said, ready to take advantage of the moment to accuse someone else of the Instigator's crash. "*You* brought the ship here?"

"What?" Khiry demanded.

"Look here," Jay started, but there was no stopping the fight.

Accusations flew. Electra's gorgeous amber eyes flashed at Gibson. His Nazi-Germany features glowed red with anger as he placed blame squarely on her. It was a USPS practice she should have been familiar with, he said, placing blame. Nothing happens without someone to blame it on. Nothing happens without someone to punish for it.

The yelling could have attracted half the mountainside's man-beasts if they'd been awake and moving about in the daylight. Khiry decided it was a pretty good test of their "nocturnal-only" tendencies.

"Could we stop this?" Kor finally hissed. He turned on Gibson. "Why would you set a course for Pangaea?"

Gibson stared for a moment, thinking up a good lie. Before he could get it out, Jay scoffed at him, "Were you in on abducting the dragons, you brownspotter? Are you culpable for that dragon's death?"

"No! Look, I put in the course for Pangaea because I was following orders."

"God, save us," Khiry said. "Where have we heard that before? That's the oldest excuse in history."

"It would appear this crew is falling apart," a male transport said to Electra. "Perhaps you should take control of this operation. You know the planet. You have our best interests in mind. You're not warring with anyone here."

"She's warring with everyone here!" Jay verbally pounced on the man. "She's the sister of Presidente La—"

"I know whose sister she is, you melon. That's why she's the most qualified to lead us."

"Who are you?" Kor asked the man.

The transport stood up a little straighter. "Daniel Kent. My family hails from the Malagasy Republic on Earth. After it sank in 2049, we relocated to the inner reaches of restructured Mozambique. I am a proud and intelligent man, Mr. Kor. I have valid ideas and this one will save us all much time and arguing along our journey."

"I've no doubt. Now, Mr. Kent, my name is John Ashley McCormick the third."

One of the other transports gasped. Khiry smiled with pride. She only flew with the best marksmen.

"No doubt you'll recognize my family name so I don't need to tell you from where I hail. I too am a proud and intelligent man. I'm also a skilled and trained killer. I have valid ideas and this one will save you a lot of time and anguish. Don't assume jurisdiction over the crew of the Instigator. You're a paid transport, not a voting member of some parliament or a dictator who can appoint leaders' sisters to go for a jolly old romp across unfamiliar planets. Electra," he turned to her, ignoring the simmering Mr. Kent and the blanching security chief.

Gibson had never known Kor's heritage. He didn't know Kor was short for McCormick. Didn't someone named McCormick go by "Mac?" He had a son of John Ashley McCormick sniffing around the treasure he'd stowed aboard the Instigator? This would not do.

Addressing Electra, Kor asked, "Would it be beneficial for us to have you lead us to the city we saw when we flew over yesterday?"

The lovely lady smiled gracefully. She bowed her head in deference to Mr. Kent, and then to Kor. "Gentlemen, you're both proud and useful men in the fight for our lives here on Eldora Prime. Don't for a minute think that I take your presence or your service for granted. I know how important you both are. Daniel Kent, you honor me by asking if I can lead this group to safety. John McCormick, you honor me, and Mr. Kent, by pursuing the idea.

"I have to admit that I know only a little about Eldora Prime. I'm more familiar with Eldora Moon. If we were there, ah, I could be so much more useful to us. I'm sorry. Here, I will give you every bit of information I can. I'll hold nothing back because all I have to give will help us all in this journey. But you have all made a wise decision to let Khiry and Kor lead us out this morning and toward the city. They saw the city as we flew over yesterday and they know the direction to go. Let's learn as we go and work together to keep each other as safe as we can."

"Now that's a politician," Jay whispered to Red.

The pale woman cradled her stubby arm to her chest, not ready to joke about anything yet. She merely stared at Jay as if she hadn't heard him.

"Well said," Mr. Kent announced. He held out his hand to Kor. "I apologize for jumping to the wrong conclusion about you and this party. I didn't realize I was in the presence of so much greatness."

Kor accepted the man's hand, because it would have been incredibly rude not to, but his tight smile spoke volumes. He didn't think the man was sorry. He didn't think that would be the man's last barbed comment.

"Let's get moving then," Gibson said. "Enough of this political crap."

That's when the journey's onset hit its big snag.

*　　　*　　　*

The dragons didn't want to leave their dead companion. At least not yet. The young dragon still mewled its pitiful cries, which had varied in volume, but remained incessant through the night.

"They're not coming?" Gibson asked in disbelief. "After we released them? After we tried to save their companion? What gratitude is that?"

Khiry wanted to backhand him.

"This isn't the mouse removing the thorn from the lion's paw," she said.

No one in the group caught her reference, least of all Gibson.

"We can't expect these alien creatures to go off and leave their dead companion unburied. But what do we know about real dragons? Nothing."

"It's like the elephants," Red murmured.

Few heard her. Fewer understood.

"We have to let them deal with their loss in their own way," Shayla agreed.

"Then we go on without them for an escort?" Gibson said. "Oh, that's just great. And what happens tonight when those beasts come after us? How many of us have to get picked off out of these makeshift little tents of Kor's before we realize we needed the dragons to protect us?"

"You have me to protect you, Chief," Kor said pointedly. His comment and reminder of the security chief's title closed the subject.

They had barely finished their latest bickering when they noticed the dragons had formed a line next to their dead companion on the grass next to the ship. Onyx took his powerful front claw and drew a line down the dead one's chest with one of his obsidian dark nails. Blood no longer flowed, no longer pooled to the surface of the dragon's body.

"What are they doing?" a transport asked.

No one answered her because no one knew for sure. Several people gasped, though, when Onyx plunged his claw into the dragon's chest. Shayla cringed and turned away. Onyx pulled out the dragon's still heart and handed it down to the young dragon. It howled in despair but accepted the token. Still emitting his pitiful cries, the smaller creature held the muscle in both front claws, tearing at it with his sharp teeth, eating it as quickly as he could. He finished the ceremony as quickly as possible, still mewling all the while. When he was done, he looked up at Onyx as if for approval.

The three adult dragons reared back their heads and roared forth spouts of orange-red flame, dousing their dead companion with a dragon funeral pyre. The younger one was only half an adult's size. He wasn't tiny. Apparently, that was small enough to be too young to produce flame. He tried. He tried to do his part, rearing his head back and spewing gaseous fume toward the growing blaze that caught at the dragon scales and flesh, searing wing and meat and sending the burnt smell over the breeze toward the party on the grass.

With their eyes fixed intently on the dragon ceremony, no one in the group noticed a trail of dust rising to their north. With their ears full of dragons' roaring and crackling fire, no one heard the hum and whir of two solar-powered vehicles puttering over rocky terrain to reach them. It wasn't until a human yelled, "Hello! You there!" that they spun, almost as one, to see someone waving frantically from the passenger seat of a roofless buggy.

Chapter Ten

"My name is Rewk," the brunette said, hopping down from the tall buggy as if it were on fire. Both vehicles looked like something out of the new Everglades back on Earth, complete with green and olive camouflage markings that Khiry would have questioned twenty-four hours earlier. As things stood, she silently applauded the idea of hiding something so useful from the strong and evil creatures on the planet.

"We don't have much time," Rewk announced. No one would mistake the urgency in her voice. "And I don't know how much it will slow us to bring this many back, but we can't leave you out here. There's a storm coming over the mountains. Once it hits, these buggies won't work and these hills will be swarming with the touched and the inhabitants."

Khiry looked toward the mountains, her gaze sweeping over the rolling foothills of grasses and crags and jutting rocks to the larger hills and finally mountains beyond. She could have mistaken it for a scene in Tennessee on Earth. Beautiful and lush and promising to hold any number of harmless creatures like deer or rabbits. Squirrels, maybe.

Instead, she had to remind herself that these mountains contained human-looking creatures that could lift a heavy-set woman up to their oversized mouths and rip her internal organs out while she screamed and squirmed for her life. These mountains may have been picturesque with their varied hues of green swelling over rise after rise, but where their snowcapped peaks met the clouding sky, something dark and foreboding sat in mockery of the grace of nature. Some evil puppet master sent nasty beasts out to feast on travelers like her crew. She wondered if the nasty beasts had already eaten all the harmless creatures like deer or rabbits. Or squirrels.

"Who's your leader?" Rewk asked, startling Khiry back to the seriousness of the moment.

A few pointed at Khiry, who stepped up to the woman. Rewk reached out and shook Khiry's hand vigorously. Her eyes looked dull and listless, despite the energized handshake. It was difficult to tell what color they used to be. Brown? Her dark complexion spoke of something Middle Eastern on Earth. Khiry wondered if that would explain the woman's long dark skirt covering even darker leggings. Long dark sleeves covered her arms. It seemed excessive in the heat of the climbing sun.

"Do you want to run for the city or do you want to hole up here for the rest of the morning? The storms generally move through quickly."

Khiry liked the idea of staying put and getting information before jumping into these unreliable buggies and depending on strangers to get them to a city that might or might not offer them the protection they needed from the beasts they'd seen the night before. Who ever heard of a solar-powered vehicle without back-up power? A storm would render them helpless.

"Let's hole up here in our cargo hold. We can be guaranteed safety while the storm passes. Do you need to bring your buggies up close to the ship?"

Rewk nodded, but her attention was no longer on Khiry. She looked past the woman, beyond the little crowd of travelers to a company of dragons moving toward them with a bonfire blazing behind them. "I assume you're aware of these dragons and have no fear of them."

Khiry smiled cautiously. "They're uneasy allies. They'll shelter with us."

Rewk raised an eyebrow in surprise. "Interesting." She turned to her compatriots in the two buggies and issued a few quick orders.

Within minutes, everyone understood that they had to get back inside to ensure their safety. On their way in, Khiry pulled Electra aside. "Are you all right with us using your name? We can introduce you as someone else."

Electra smiled and placed a hand on Khiry's arm. "You're kind to worry about me. Use my name. I think it will help us."

Rewk had waited as long as her nerves would allow and stepped up to get Khiry's attention again. "Do you still have communications? Have you called for help?"

"Nothing. Communications were on the bridge, which is…" she gestured to the landscape around them, indicating "everywhere."

Rewk couldn't hide her disappointment.

"What about power?" one of the men with Rewk asked. "Does your ship have power coils?"

Khiry saw nothing odd about his question, but Gibson turned a glare on them. "What business is that of yours?"

"Shut up, Gibson," Khiry said. "Help everyone to the hold." She looked back at their guests. "Please ignore him. He's our security officer and he gets a little nervous around new people." She wasn't sure why she felt the need to lie for the rude guy. "The Instigator has two power coils. If they weren't damaged in the crash, they should have at least half their life in them. Do you think we can get them to the city in your buggies? They'll do no good here."

"Oh, yes," Rewk breathed. "Bilal, have someone show you where they are."

"Engineering, of course," Khiry said. "But the storm's so close."

"No time like the present," the young man named Bilal said. "And no point wasting any daylight any time. You'll learn that fast here on Eldora Prime."

*   *   *

The storm hit the ship with hurricane force. As if trying to set them at ease, trying to make small talk, one of Rewk's traveling companions spoke kindly to the obviously injured and frightened Red. It was Bilal and he offered a stark contrast to her ruddy, plump, quiet countenance. He was sun-tanned, thin and tone, and spoke with a confident voice for his age.

"We saw you fly over the city yesterday so close to dusk that we didn't dare to set out to find you. We could only pray that you had enough of your ship still together that you could hole up overnight. Stay warm and safe from the bad things that come out at night."

Rewk's other companion, a thicker, burlier, bearded man named Seek chimed in. "We set out this morning as soon as the sun hit the buggies." He worked with antiseptic and bandages from a first-aid kit Rewk had carried into the hold to doctor Khiry's hand while they spoke. "Took us no time to find you."

"No time?" Jay asked. "How long is that, exactly?"

"What would you say, Bilal? Two hours? From sunup to here. It's about a hundred and twenty kilometers. Maybe less. Not far past one of our mines so there's a road most of the way."

Shayla frowned and leaned toward Jay at her side. "I don't know how far that is."

"One hundred and twenty kilometers is about seventy-five miles."

She nodded. "Thank you."

A new gale force wind pummeled the ship with howling frenzy. Onyx sat up on his haunches to overlook the council before him. Khiry could feel his trepidation. She frowned at their new guests. "Do you think this ship will withstand these winds?"

Rewk nodded solemnly. "We've prayed already."

Gibson ran his hand down his face, glancing nervously at Khiry. Then he glared at the leader opposite her. "You've prayed about it? And how often do these storms knock down buildings in your city?"

"Very rarely," Rewk said with a knowing smile. "The buildings we've erected in Touch Down City are made of steel similar to that used in this ship's hull. Quality steel from Earth."

"So how often is 'very rarely'?" Kor asked.

Rewk gave him a condescending smile. It seemed everyone from the Instigator crash site hung on her words now. "There's no need to worry. The storms that have caused damage to the outlying buildings of Touch Down City come in the winter. This is our summer season. We've been terraforming here nearly two decades. In that time, we've built a solid, self-sustaining city from the parts delivered from Earth and from the minerals and elements we've mined here." She looked at Khiry directly. "I know this sector of Eldora Prime well, Khiry Okerson. Your people are quite safe in this structure during a summer squall. Once it passes, we'll have plenty of afternoon sun to power us back to Touch Down City well before darkness descends."

"Your words are comforting," Khiry said, thinking it sounded like something Electra would say. "Could you tell us a bit about what happens when darkness descends?"

Rewk smiled again—one of those knowing smiles that a mother bestows on a child who's asked an embarrassing question in public. "Is that something to discuss so openly?"

"We're all adults here and have no secrets to hide," Khiry said. "We're not voting on what choices to make, but we're all going into this journey with our eyes open."

Rewk nodded, as if she thought that was fine for this little group. She then let her eyes light on Shayla. "It just seems that some might be troubled by too much honesty."

Ah, found our weakest link so easily, Khiry thought. "We share and discuss that honesty as we need to."

Rewk nodded again. "All right. When darkness comes. First, you no doubt noticed that the temperature drops considerably here at night. Eldora Moon where you came from doesn't experience such extremes. By day, in the season we call 'summer' for lack of any better term, the days reach temperatures of thirty-two to thirty-five degrees Celsius."

Shayla leaned over to Jay. "I don't know what that is."

"About ninety to ninety-five Fahrenheit."

She nodded.

"At the heart of night, the temperature has dipped to four to ten degrees Celsius," Rewk continued.

"About forty to fifty," Jay translated for Shayla.

She smiled shyly at him and mouthed, "thank you."

"As summer moves toward winter, the daylight becomes shorter, as it is in certain regions of Earth," Rewk continued. "In this sector of Eldora Prime, the longest summer day has been ten Earth hours. The shortest has been four Earth hours. Yes, I see your surprise. We were surprised as well, the first few years. The cold snaps provide excellent preparation for summer crops, we've found. And the cold snaps kill off all manner of insects and even some mammalian pests. What the cold has not killed off is the creature we call the inhabitants. Apparently you met with these beasts last night?"

"I think so," Khiry said, hoping there was only one demonesque creature to deal with here. "The man-beasts with the bulging eyes? They unhook their jaws to eat their prey?"

Rewk shook her head sadly. "I'm afraid that isn't an inhabitant."

Smear it, Khiry thought.

"What you describe is one of the touched," Rewk said. "It's one of our people. A human who's been taken by an inhabitant and…well…for lack of a better term…turned to something inhuman. We refer to them as the touched. We haven't found a way to save one of these people once they've been turned. We've tried. They're nearly impossible to capture. At least, nearly impossible to hold in captivity. I suppose you noticed its inhuman strength? That's a trait of the inhabitants that gets passed on to the touched when the inhabitants leave one alive. They're strong, fast, cunning, heavy, insatiable. They have those mouths like you describe—the jaws come unhinged and this set of teeth comes forward and bites…"

Her voice trailed off for a moment while they all stared at her in stunned silence. It was as if she told a ghost story around a campfire. Surely this wasn't true.

"The bite of an inhabitant delivers a toxin that turns the human. If the inhabitant doesn't finish you off—eating your fatty tissues and organs, which seem to be the only parts they desire—then you eventually regain consciousness as one of the touched. Then that insatiable hunger is yours. Yet…yet I've seen the touched attack a human and leave him or her to awake as a touched. It's as if they intend to pass on some virus from the inhabitants until we're all transformed."

One of the transports wiped tears from her eyes.

"The inhabitants move about on all eight legs and run like the wind when they get something in their sights," Rewk continued. "They have trouble during the day because the light hurts their eyes. As you said, the beasts you saw have bulging eyes. This is true for the inhabitants as well. They live in the caves in the mountains." She paused as if afraid to tell them any more. "That's where we found them." She gave a weak smile. "We built a road from Touch Down City to the mines before we hit the veins that opened up and spilled forth these creatures. You have to be careful when mining a new planet. God only knows what you'll wake when you drill beneath the surface of a new world."

Everyone was quiet for a few minutes as if they expected her to say more. Finally, Khiry cleared her throat softly and asked, "How do you kill an inhabitant?"

"Any plasma weapon to the abdomen or head. Radiator weapons work, too. Flame throwers. Knives if you're in a tight spot, but, really, it's best to avoid tight spots when it comes to an inhabitant."

Khiry and Kor nodded in unison.

"And how do you kill a touched?" she asked next.

Rewk looked a little uncomfortable at this. "We don't like doing that."

"I beg your pardon?" Gibson asked.

"They're our people. Family and friends. Co-workers, colleagues, spouses, neighbors. Children. It's not easy to take up a weapon against a loved one."

"Yes, but they're changed," Khiry said.

"Not entirely. You can tell they have some memory in them…some idea of who they used to be. They come back for their own families."

Khiry shuddered. "That's horrific. You must want to put them out of their misery, out of that new and horrid existence. I mean, when you're put to it, what works?" Khiry asked. "What saves you from becoming a touched like them?"

Rewk sighed. "All the same things we use on the inhabitants. Only…you can also drown a touched. I learned that the hard way." She looked sickened by the thought.

"All right then," Khiry said. "Enough of that talk. How have you fortified the city against these inhabitants?"

"We've built a wall around the city. We buried landmines in the fields immediately around the outlying farmland and in a perimeter around the city."

"Landmines!" Electra said in disbelief. "You can't be serious."

"I know your brother would be disappointed to hear it, but we had no choice. There's a drawbridge into the city. All of us know of the landmines and where they are. We're perfectly safe."

"Glad we didn't land there," Kor said to Khiry.

She shot him an annoyed glance. There was more to this Touch Down City that irritated her than landmines. A drawbridge? People hesitant to kill an enemy? Mining until you wake an indigenous population that you couldn't control or eradicate? What kind of mess was this planet in? And why hadn't they sent for help?

Chapter Eleven

Khiry didn't get to ask any of her questions. Her thoughts were interrupted by a scratching at the outside of the cargo hold. Onyx lifted his massive head and glared at the door as if he could see through it to whatever clamored for their attention outside. Khiry glanced at him as she gathered Shayla up out of the floor. She didn't know—maybe dragons could see through walls. Who knew what kind of vision they had.

"Stay with Junior," Khiry told Shayla. "Protect him."

Shayla took the weapon Khiry pressed into her hand and pulled the young dragon toward the damaged cage, away from the door where evil knocked. The poor thing still looked depressed, but this new danger and the reactions of every living thing in the cargo hold put him on high alert. He looked to Shayla, somehow grasping that she was there to guard him. T-Rex barked a dragon command at him. He was to protect the human. Neither understood that they'd been given their orders merely to keep them from worrying about themselves when the inevitable attack came. Their orders were to stave off their own fears.

Rewk looked to her men. "Inhabitants or touched?"

"Sounds like touched," Bilal offered. "I hear voices on the wind."

Rewk swore. "Well, we must do what we must, my friends."

The two nodded.

"What do you think?" Khiry asked Kor. Gibson, Trane, and Electra stood in their tight circle, Jay and Mr. Kent rushing in to hear what orders would be given.

"I think they're going to find a way in with this storm at their backs," Kor said. "The storm came from the north and that's the direction of the city. If we run far enough, we could run out of storm and into the sun."

Rewk overheard him. "That's madness. They'd catch you in a heartbeat."

"Not all of us," Gibson said.

"Who do you sacrifice?" Rewk snapped back.

"*I'm* not suggesting anyone be sacrificed," Kor said, tossing a menacing glare at Gibson. "I can kill a dozen of these things by myself."

Seek snorted. "You can say what you want to comfort the ladies, but you'll be useless to them if you're dead, and these creatures will turn and chase them down."

Kor turned back to Khiry's group, ignoring Seek's cynical advice. "Does everyone have light?"

"Light?" Mr. Kent asked.

"Everyone should take at least one flashlight. LED. This hold's full of them. If you can get more, take more in your belt. The city's one hundred and twenty kilometers from here. That'll take nearly forty hours to walk so we want to walk very fast. Shayla,"

She stood in her place, but listened intently. "Yes."

"Why do you stick to the road? The path of the buggies?" he asked her, quizzing her.

The young lady stared for a moment, caught in the stare of all those people and four dragons. "The path. We stick to the path…" It suddenly dawned on her. "Because of the landmines."

"Good girl. Stay on the path and shine those LEDs in the eyes of anything that gets in your way. Stab it, shoot it, burn it alive. Understood?"

Everyone in the hold nodded.

Khiry felt her stomach turn over itself. This was it. Kor was talking about going out into the dusk of a storm with those creatures that wanted to eat them. She was going to die on an alien planet because her stupid captain had stolen heavy dragons from their home. Or so she believed. She turned to Rewk.

"What protects us once we're in the city?"

"We have weapons," Rewk answered.

"What powers them?"

Rewk hadn't expected that question. "What?"

"They're not solar powered or you'd be defenseless at night. What powers them?"

"We have the power coils," Bilal said.

Gibson visibly flinched, drawing Kor's attention away from the door where he'd been trying to count voices and footsteps on the other side.

"We also use nuclear power," Seek offered.

"Nuclear power? Here? With what?" Jay asked.

Of course the science and computer nerd would ask that, Khiry thought.

"We mine an element from the mountains here with the exact properties of Uranium-235," Rewk said. "It powers the fission reaction perfectly."

Khiry frowned. "So you mined this element before you found the inhabitants? Before they woke?"

"Yes. Why?"

"How did you know you needed it?" Khiry asked.

"I don't understand," Rewk said.

"What were you doing mining a Uranium-235-like element before you needed to provide nuclear power to protect your city from inhabitants? You didn't know about the inhabitants yet."

Bilal raised a hand to stop Rewk from answering in anger. "You misunderstand us," he said. "You think we were making weapons, don't you? Rest assured, we just wanted nuclear power. We use small nuclear reactors in our vessels to power the rockets. You've heard of water electrolysis-based rockets? They require enormous water tanks and small nuclear reactors."

Gibson nodded all the while during this part of Bilal's speech. No one could have guessed he put plans in motion for stealing one of the terraformers' ships. Who would think he had a reason to get off the planet without the rest of the group?

"Trust me," Bilal continued, "our motives were pure and simple. The inhabitants have forced us into a defensive mode. Please, let's deal with the immediate problem. Let's defend this hold until the storm passes if we possibly can. Then let's get everyone safely to the city where we can speak calmly and at length."

Spoken like Electra, Khiry thought. She could learn much about leading from the people around her. If she survived the "immediate problem," as Bilal called it.

The immediate problem had found a way to drive its prey out into the open. A number of the touched stood outside the ship, just beyond the wall where the cargo hold door stood as their only barrier. And they pushed.

They pushed against the ship to tip the section containing their prey over on its side. The rocking motion betrayed their plan.

"They're organized and intelligent," Kor said to Khiry.

The two stood next to the door, listening to what appeared to be a leader's call outside. She looked up into his dark brown eyes, lost for a second in the pools of liquid chocolate like something you'd find in a delicatessen on Earth. She felt the color rise to her cheeks. Whether they made up a good marksman or not, this was no time to think about a colleague's finer features.

He smiled at her as if he read her distracted thought. "We should gather everyone by the far wall." He jerked his head toward the other wall as if she should mistake which one he meant and his dark brown locks tousled with the movement. "When they tip us over, there'll be fewer injuries."

She nodded. "Wise."

He almost said something else, but she'd already turned, saying, "All right, everyone, they're going to tip us this direction. Gather over here and we'll be safer. Come on." She used a sweeping motion with her arms, gesturing with her flashlight in one hand and a plasma gun in the other as she herded everyone, including dragons, toward the far wall.

"You don't think we can stop their plan if we put all the weight against that wall?" Gibson said, pointing toward the door.

"Even with the dragons, I doubt it," Kor said. "They're determined and strong. It sounds like quite a number of them working at it." He had moved away from the wall and swept the exposed portions of the floor with a raptor gaze, searching for imperfections, tears, holes, anything that would let one of the monsters through once the simple metal floor became a wall.

"That would have to be *quite* a number—"

Khiry interrupted Gibson to keep him from sending everyone into a panic. "Does everyone have a flashlight and a weapon?" She knew *just* what kind of army it would take to tip this ship with four dragons and fifteen people standing on the panels the army intended to move. It made her stomach flop again.

Onyx stared at her as if waiting for her to give another command. She smiled as best she could and he made some garbled sound that she assumed was encouragement. Then the ship rocked again, tipping up, up, up ninety degrees.

Chapter Twelve

The chaos of people screaming and objects falling rattled Khiry's nerves, but she couldn't let herself get lost in emotions. These people depended on her. Sure it was supposed to be Gibson's job to protect the crew and the transports the Instigator took on, but Gibson wasn't one to step up and take responsibility for anyone's life but his own. Even then he seemed to shirk his duty in favor of letting someone in power make his health and welfare decisions for him. It would get him an early death sentence some day.

They hadn't had time to move crates and boxes. Each person just had to dodge the falling bombs as the hold tilted to its new resting point. One of the transports found himself lodged between a couple of the standing bars of the dragon's former cage and a crate that quite obviously crushed his leg. The man screamed like a little girl, not just because it hurt, but because he was afraid. "Don't leave me here!" he screamed. "Don't leave me here for them!"

"Shut up!" Gibson snapped, helping Mr. Kent lug the crate off the man. Khiry appreciated Gibson getting the transport to stop his unnerving yelps, but it seemed an unkind way to do it. Maybe a swift kick to the head would have made a good example of the man; and would have solved a problem. The nature of his injury made him dead weight. Khiry wondered briefly if Maas would have taken responsibility for the transport's safety if she'd survived last night.

Something heavy landed on the wall-turned-ceiling next to the door-turned-escape-hatch. Khiry and Kor exchanged worried glances. "That's our way out," he said.

"Unless we torch our way through somewhere else," she suggested.

He snapped his fingers. "That's the best plan I've heard since the mess hall," he tossed over his shoulder, pulling the enormous plasma streamer gun from its carrier on his back. He set it on maximum and scooted into the dragon cage. "Better defense," he called behind him.

Rewk and her men nodded at the wisdom. "Help him," she ordered Bilal.

With the powerful weapon, it took no time at all to get through the wall, revealing a hall that they could only hope led to a free passage to the open road where no hostiles watched. The sound of crunching metal reached them. It was like fingernails on an old Earth chalkboard.

"Beautiful. They're *eating* their way in," Gibson muttered.

"Maybe they'll wear those teeth down to nubs," Seek shouted, pointing his weapon at the holes forming near the door in the ceiling.

"Let's go!" Kor called from the dragon cage. He'd made a hole big enough for the dragons to squeeze through. It would be difficult to defend; it was imperative they get out quickly. "Women and children right after Bilal."

Shayla and her dragon friend scrambled toward the opening. Kor shook his head slightly as she scurried past him. He stroked her curly red hair as she darted out the cargo hold right behind the young dragon. He figured he'd never see her again. If one of the "touched" got hold of him, he certainly hoped he never saw her again.

Red and Seek were next. "I'll get her there safe and sound," Seek said. He didn't realize that, before Red's accident, no one aboard the Instigator had cared much for the obnoxious tighter. Right now she had their pity in spades. She couldn't have planned a better accident to get a safe escort to Touch Down City.

As the first touched creature fell through the hole in the ceiling, Jay pulled Khiry through the hole in the wall and into the hall with Onyx squishing in behind them. Kor turned and blasted the man-beast with a shot from the plasma streamer canon. It left a splatter of man-matter where the beast had stood just a second before. The next beast preparing to drop through the hole hesitated, letting out a squall that bordered on hellish.

*   *   *   *   *

One by one or in groups of two or three, the party spilled out an opening in the ship's hull into a torrent of rain. The scent of rainfall and wet earth surprised the crew of the Instigator with its familiarity. Eldora Prime smelled like home when a summer storm drummed her mountains and swelled her streams with cold water.

From crew members to terraformers, each of them experienced the shock of having the wind press his or her breath back in his or her throat, making it difficult to do more than gasp in a mouthful of rainwater at first.

The young dragon tossed his head in confusion and fear. He'd never felt the sensation of drowning on his own breath before. Shayla moved to stand between him and the driving blast, turning her back to the storm. With his head down, he could use her body to shelter against the immediate onslaught and rake in a frantic lungful of air. She held onto him for a moment, letting him breathe until Jay's hands grabbed her shoulders and they were on the move across the countryside. Running. Running fast as if demons chased them.

The first to fall, of course, was the injured transport. Gibson and Mr. Kent literally dropped him in the slopping mud as they trailed the group. The man let out a squeal of terror, but the squeal was all the touched allowed him. They were that close on the group's heals. Gibson fired into the mass, running backward, slipping and sliding, trying to maintain footing as Mr. Kent stumbled alongside him.

The touched that hadn't stopped for the transport were catching up easily. The man-beasts ran swiftly for creatures with so much mass. Their weight made them appear solid and fearsome, but also made their steps sink in the mud. Each lift of a foot had an accompanying schluck-and-pop sound that could sometimes be heard over their wailing and gnashing of jagged, ugly teeth. As they flailed their arms to keep their balance on the sloppy terrain, the creatures howled and hooted to their comrades, giving directions for the chase.

With a curse, Gibson reached one hand for Kent's flashlight hand.

"What?" Mr. Kent began. His eyes went wide in worry, and then narrowed to slits in anger as he realized what Gibson intended. He tried to yank his arm away. He lost his footing.

Gibson's fingers closed around the end of the flashlight and pulled as Kent went down. He turned and ran for broke to the sounds of Kent screaming profanities at him, to the sound of the man's blood gurgling up in his throat as the creatures pounced quickly. As he ran, he passed the terraformer named Seek face-down in the mud. *I'm not stopping,* he thought. Seek didn't appear to be moving. Maybe he was already dead. He counted the seconds until he heard him screaming, using that to gauge how close the touched were behind him.

That's when he noticed the dragons. They were flying in the storm. *Blast it! I should've befriended one of the larger beasts,* he thought. The one Khiry referred to as T-Rex carried Red in one of its claws and flew with her toward the light beyond the storm clouds ahead. He could see the other two adult dragons carrying people as well, getting them one by one to the safety so close in the near distance. He waved his arms then as he ran, calling, "Hey! Take me, too! Take me next!"

He had nearly reached the road the terraformers had talked about, had nearly come out of the mud-and-grass part of this ordeal. By the time he ran all the way to the sunlit landscape a few kilometers ahead, he was winded and angry. No dragon had come back for him. Not even the small one who'd apparently struggled carrying Shayla. The group walked at an even pace by then, comforting each other, assessing their wounds and condition as they moved. They wouldn't dare stop, but afforded a reasonable pace to recover from the crisis they'd just survived. Their footsteps didn't drag yet, but moved with the weight of those with heavy, troubled thoughts. The dragons' steps were naturally heavy, causing the ground to shake as the four moved in an unsteady rhythm next to the road.

Once Gibson caught his breath, he grumbled to Kor, "Thanks for nothing."

The warrior stared back at him. "I think you need to think about your character," Kor said. "The dragons know a man's soul. They saved everyone they felt was worth saving. What's in you, Gibson, that makes you not worth saving?"

Kor didn't speak loudly. This wasn't something for the entire company to hear.

"You're serious!" Gibson said in shock.

"Deadly so. Re-evaluate yourself. It may be time to change who you are at the core."

Gibson's teeth ground together against the desire to kill the man right there, out in the open light of day in front of all these people. So what if they needed his skill as a marksman to get safely to Touch Down City? Kor had so deeply offended Gibson that the affront wouldn't be soon forgotten. Gibson closed his mouth and considered how it would serve them all right if the dragons walking beside the road stepped on landmines.

Onyx didn't stop walking, but turned his regal black head back to look Gibson full in the eyes. The dragon seemed to snarl.

Chapter Thirteen

When only two or so hours remained before darkness and all nature of inhumanity would descend upon them, Khiry asked Rewk what she thought of hiding the party for the night among the outcroppings of rocks that made up the foothills of the mountains.

"I don't know that we'll find something large enough for your dragons to fit in," Rewk answered.

"We could send them ahead," Kor suggested.

Rewk shook her head. "I don't know that the folks at the city would welcome four unexpected dragons flying in in the dead of night."

"So we send you in Onyx's grasp," Khiry said, matter of factly. "If he's bringing you home, surely they won't shoot him out of the sky. And you can explain what's happening. The rest of us come along tomorrow."

"It would be close to dusk by the time we get there, but we should make it by tomorrow if we keep up a good pace," Bilal estimated. "We ran a good distance this morning. And we picked up the pace early on after that. I'd say we've walked at more than three kilometers per Earth hour all afternoon."

"You're talking about covering seventy-five miles in less than two days of sunlight," Kor said in amazement.

"Ah, this crew can do it," Bilal announced, just loudly enough that the folks straining to overhear them overheard that. It sounded jovial.

Khiry shot him a withering glance. "You can fill their heads with nonsense, as I think someone suggested to Kor earlier, but running them into the ground until dark tomorrow night will just make them unable to fight whatever comes after them."

"By tomorrow night, they'll either be within the city's walls or reinforcements will have come out to help us. Those aren't the only buggies we own, you know."

Khiry's eyebrows arched as she considered this.

"Of course," Kor mumbled. "You wouldn't have risked all your powered vehicles at once."

"If there's hope, then," Khiry thought out loud. "These others just might be convinced to double this pace tomorrow. We might be able to hold them together through the night, no matter what's sniffing around their hiding spot in the dark. If there's hope that these powered vehicles can come out to greet us close to the city tomorrow evening and pull us in where it's safe, we just might get everyone to survive."

Rewk offered a weak but genuine smile. "How long have you been leading this crew?" She was about to continue with "They must love you heartily; they will follow you to the ends of Eldora Prime." But Khiry had snorted some sort of laugh that interrupted her.

"About twenty-four hours. Our captain, sot that he was, died in the crash. I assumed leadership by default."

Rewk and Bilal exchanged nervous glances. "By default?" Rewk finally asked.

"Gibson is our security chief. By all rights, he's next in the chain of command aboard our ship. But, look at him. You've seen his actions. You know his quality. That couldn't lead us."

Rewk nodded in agreement, but there was a hesitation in her agreement. Bilal stared at the ground.

"Say what you're thinking," Kor ordered them. "There's no sense in us having secrets from each other out here. We depend on each other to survive the night."

Bilal looked him in the eye. "You're right, of course."

"We think you sound a lot like resistance," Rewk said. "You've got Presidente Lamahl Endh's sister on your ship, yet you didn't give her leadership when your captain died. She sounds like a hostage to a renegade band of jumpers who've got alien dragons for allies. You crashed here on your way back to Earth with these dragons. Were they a gift to the resistance blenders?"

Khiry's jaw dropped open. What an inane theory! Kor reached up to scratch the right side of his beard with the knife no one had seen him palm. "We're not jumpers," he said calmly. His voice was all reassurance.

"We might accuse *you* of being jumpers," Khiry said, surprised at how calmly the words passed her lips. "You may pose as terraformers, but what colonists worth their salt would forego signaling for help when something as hideous and dangerous as these inhabitants showed up stealing from your population? Wouldn't you naturally send for help from the USPS?"

Rewk sighed. "We tried. Who knows what happened to our first few messages to Earth, but our communications systems have been destroyed and our power coils used up for other purposes. We use every last ounce of power and technology we have for defense now. A team works to get our transport vessel ready for interstellar travel. If we could even get to Eldora Moon we could alert someone to what's happening here."

Khiry watched not just the dark woman, but also her bodyguard. "And that's the truth? You've been on this planet's surface for two decades and couldn't fix a ship or a communications system in all that time?"

"We've not been under attack that whole time," Bilal explained. "And the attacks have required we focus considerable energy—"

"And manpower," she interjected.

"And manpower on staying alive. We've built a wall around a city and installed a drawbridge while defending it and awaiting orders from Earth. After our first call for help, we expected a response. When the response didn't come before our communications were destroyed, we expected reinforcements. When reinforcements didn't come, we didn't know what to expect. We had to do something. Now that you've arrived and it's obvious you're not an armada from the USPS sent to rescue us, we have to figure out your motives for ourselves. It's just natural that we'd see you carrying Electra Endh and jump to some conclusions."

"Maybe," Khiry said. "But it makes no sense to me that the USPS would send you here, lose communication with you, and never check in. Eldora Moon is less than half a million miles away. They could have sent a ship by to check on you on a whim at least once in twenty years…"

While her voice trailed and she wondered what point she tried to make, Rewk nodded. "I see what you're trying to say. You want to know why someone didn't try contacting us. We couldn't get a message to Earth; why didn't Earth try getting a message to us when our communications stopped? Truly, I don't know. All I can think is that it would be most inconvenient for Presidente Endh to learn that his terraformers have failed here. Ever since the United States space community received permission from their president to find habitable planets in the summer of 2009, the entire world's space community has been joined in the mission to get as many humans off Earth as possible. We weren't just scarring that planet's surface; we were contributing to its warming by infinitely increasing percentages of temperatures with each passing year. Presidente Endh has united leaders, dictators, presidents, kings…you name it…in this mission to terraform out here among the stars. This can't be news to you. But to have one of the few colonies that was succeeding early on suddenly call in with such dire news, to say that we didn't spend enough time researching the planet we considered habitable…it suggests he's moved too quickly to offload the populace."

They paused at the end of her speech. Electra, listening from a few meters away, seethed, but no one noticed her. And no one would have known if she flushed in anger over hearing her brother's sins laid bare or over her embarrassment at their validity.

"So you see why we doubted your motives?" Rewk said gently. "We didn't know if you were USPS officers sent to save us or sent to finish us off to prevent a recording of the Presidente's failure. When it was apparent this wasn't a USPS vessel, we thought you might be resistance."

Kor cleared his throat. He didn't want to minimize their plight, but he wanted to assure them somehow. "I can set your minds to rest. I'm John Ashley McCormick the third. I would never—"

He paused for his audience to recover their breath.

"I would never sully my family's name by putting in with an unworthy cause. You know the McCormicks have fought to defend the USPS's family many times over the decades. Our captain is the idiot who snuck dragons on board the ship without anyone knowing. He's the one who committed treason against the USPS. Now Khiry has to get that message across to the USPS for us. She's a good leader for this crew. She offered to hand that role to Electra, and Electra turned it down because she doesn't know the lay of the land here. She offered to help us work with the terraformers if and when we found you. So far, we haven't had much opportunity to sit down and work. Fighting for our lives kinda takes precedence."

Bilal snickered at that. "You've got a number of leaders in your group," he said to Khiry. "It's a strong unit. I'm glad you're adding to our number."

She hoped her face didn't betray her reticence. She looked over at the group seated not far from them. The young dragon and Shayla was their weakest link. Then there was Red. Who knew when that bomb was going to go off? The two surviving transports—one a woman prone to fainting and one a man who looked far along in years—didn't seem too promising. Gibson could only be trusted to fight for his own life. Jay and Trane were worth their salt. She had no doubt they'd do all they could to help keep the others safe. And she felt pretty confident the dragons would, too, if Onyx let the two adults stay when he took Rewk back to the city. Of course, this all depended on her getting their plan across to a dragon from Eldora Moon.

In all, eleven people and four dragons to fight off the impending horrors of the night. Well, ten people and two-and-a-half dragons if Onyx went along with the plan.

*　*　*　*　*

Khiry and Rewk stood a ways apart from the group, where the little pod of dragons stood as if guarding them. Khiry used a great deal of hand signals, a lot of pointing and flapping of her arms, to give her message to Onyx. The regal black dragon watched with his wise gray-blue eyes.

He understood her completely. The human she pointed to needed to get to another location, quickly, by flying. It appeared that his favorite human wanted him to take the female leader of the moving crates. He, of course, was not going to leave his favorite human unguarded.

From their positions a few dozen meters away, everyone watched him bow his head in a gesture of understanding.

"That's amazing," the female transport breathed.

Onyx barked an order to the lesser black dragon, who stepped forward and held out a massive claw to Rewk. She gave Bilal a half-smile. To say she was excited would be a lie, but the terraforming leader wasn't afraid, either. She'd stared nightmarish death in the face one too many times in the past dozen years for a dragon's flight to scare her.

Placing a hand on Rewk's arm to arrest her, Khiry said, "Look, I'm…I'm sorry, again, about the loss of Seek."

Rewk nodded. "Thank you. Again. It's hard to lose a good security officer, but he died in the line of duty. That will make his family proud."

Khiry winced. "Family?"

Rewk heaved a sigh. "Yes. He's got a wife of sorts back in the city. She's an alien. He was a mixer."

"You're kidding. I never would have guessed."

"Neither would we. She seems as normal as you and me. As that computer mechanic of yours."

Khiry felt a flush of concern for Jay.

"But they had a mixling that didn't survive a day. Hideous thing. I've never seen anything like it. Doctors said it had extra organs inside. Never could have made it. God knows why these mixers try such things."

Khiry didn't respond as Rewk stepped up to the lesser black dragon. Something in her wanted to say "love." While not familiar with the concept herself, she figured "love" was why anyone, Earthling, alien, dragon, or otherwise, attempted a relationship or attempted to share life within that relationship. On a planet teeming with beasts that seemed bent on nothing but howling and feeding, the concept seemed foreign. No wonder Seek's baby had died. Love didn't survive here.

Chapter Fourteen

"This chill reminds me of Christmas back home," the transport told her.

Khiry put a finger to her lips to suggest he be quiet. Instead of shutting his trap, the man lowered his voice to speak more quietly to the group huddled in the small space. He was older than she first thought, but fit for his age. His wrinkled face suggested he had a brood of grandchildren "back home" on Earth who would have appreciated this story more than the group staring at him in disbelief right then. She was pretty sure none of them wanted to hear him talking when their lives depended on silence. Was he senile? Did he not understand?

Shayla soon looked pleased to listen to his story, but, really, Shayla wasn't the sharpest tool in the box. Trane, whom she couldn't stop thinking of as "Bay," looked to Khiry as if asking permission to knock the old man over the head—or fire him out an airlock. The only other member of their hiding group was the young dragon, and even he appeared annoyed with the noise.

That was all that fit in their rocky outcropping in the mountain foothills. Two other outcroppings held other groupings of their party. Kor and Bilal guarded Electra and Red in a hollow somewhere in the dark. Jay and Gibson guarded the female transport in another. As they had planned, the lesser black dragon had carried Rewk off to Touch Down City just over an hour before.

No wild game lived in the foothills, according to Bilal, so they gave no thought to hunting something for a meal before they all disappeared into their hiding places. Kor, Trane, and Jay distributed ship's rations from their packs and sent everyone into hiding with the meager meals. Junior got two. Onyx and T-Rex sniffed at the offering, but declined to eat it. Khiry wasn't sure if they were going to find food out in the dark or not, but the two shifted into shadow to hide among boulders and wait out the night. Maybe they'd wait and eat one of the travelers tomorrow.

Until uneasy sleep claimed them, the remaining people sat in what they hoped were easily defendable clusters of worry and two-day-old sweat. While their little cluster didn't smell good, Khiry didn't care about the minor inconvenience; they were still alive. The earthiness of the dirt floor and limestone-like walls helped cover up the distinct mixes of body odor anyway. And the dragon smelled…well…like a dragon. More limestone and rock smell. It helped mask the dirty humans.

If not for the old man's low voice, she could have listened to their breathing. Instead, she had to hear a comparison of the foothills with the river basin in Missouri. She heard of its changing temperatures and temperament during the past fifty or so years. That's why he compared Christmastime back home to this setting.

"It's gotten warmer there like it used to be in Mississippi," he practically whispered. "So now when it comes on Christmas, we still have some green grass, like here. We still have cooler nights like this and the stars come out all bright and sparkly like this. But it doesn't snow like it used to in the winter. You got to go pretty far into Canada to get snow for Christmas."

Shayla smiled at him, but Khiry turned from her vigil at the cleft in the rocks to face him and whispered violently, "If you don't stop talking now, I will shoot you until you're dead and you'll never see another Christmas on Earth. Do you understand?"

The man had the audacity to look surprised.

As with the night before, the man-beasts came for them before darkness was complete. This time, the crew members of the Instigator were ready. Whether or not that made the attack easier on their nerves could be debated. No heavy ship's hull protected them tonight. Only stealth, quiet, and formations of rock and brush kept them hidden from prying, dirty fingers with missing nails and pealing flesh.

Khiry watched wide-eyed with Shayla and Junior at her back as one of the touched stood not five paces from her cleft in the rocks. The creature sniffed at the air.

They can smell us, Khiry thought.

The man-beast let out some sort of spine-chilling howl. A moment later, she saw movement near him. She couldn't see the whole creature that had arrived. Only thick, prickly legs came into view at first. They seemed tall, black in the moonlight, and jerked across her field of vision quickly. Too quickly to count. Hadn't Rewk said these things had eight legs? *Like a spider on Earth,* she thought.

She watched for more clarity, listening to the inhabitant clicking something as if imitating speech to the touched. They hovered too close to her hiding spot for comfort. Each time the touched lifted his nose into the night and breathed in a great lungful of air, she knew he honed in on their position. She knew it in her gut.

She rested her finger just below the plasma streamer's trigger. Not ready to turn it on yet, not ready for its whine to give away their exact location, she didn't press, but she waited with trembling muscles. Her breathing turned ragged while she watched the inhabitant scuttle in its alien motion across her view again. This time she thought she saw a creature man-like in abdomen but high up on the eight thick, bent legs. Khiry heard a chirping and clicking that underlay the surrounding man-beasts' yelps and howls. The dark filled with the sounds.

The touched in front of her hiding spot must have understood the inhabitant. He turned toward the cleft in the rocks, staring directly at her with his huge, bulging orbs. She gulped. Surely it couldn't see her, hidden as she was by brush and twigs and grass. So many rocks and crevices were covered like this. How could he correctly pick the one she was in?

Smell, she told herself.

The touched one moved toward her cautiously, with purpose.

Father in Heaven, give me courage, she thought, tightening her grip on the gun in her right hand. She tested the weight of the flashlight in her left hand as if making sure it had the miniature power coil that gave the LED source unlimited life. All she need do was push the button that would blind the ugly creature nearing her, but something stilled her hand. Something made her wait. Denial, perhaps.

She wasn't ready yet to believe that the creature had so easily zeroed in on her position. Surely he would turn at the last minute and check some other pile of brush; not hers. Surely he wouldn't tear the brush and grasses aside, dragging her out for the inhabitant he served to feed on her and Shayla…

Her heart pounded in her brain.

That's when Jay's barbaric yawp sounded across the foothills and the alien sprinted from out of nowhere, plasma streamer gun splattering the touched one into nothing but spewed blood and tissue.

"No you don't!" he shouted at the darkness. His flashlight sought and found the eyes of the inhabitant investigating Khiry's hiding spot as he ran toward it. His plasma gun's stream followed the light's beam, splattering guts, leg parts, eyes, and tufts of thick, sticky hair every which way.

"Stay in your places! All of you!" he shouted, running deeper into the foothills. Every dark shape that followed him wailed as if to drown out his warning. The sounds of exploding touched ones tolled his success with the plasma streamer as surely as their higher-pitched shrieks of anger. It was just a matter of time.

Khiry closed her eyes tightly, even though she could no longer see him or his beam of crisp, blue-tinted light skipping crazily across the landscape. Closing her eyes only made it worse. On the backs of her eyelids, she saw the brief illumination of the inhabitant's face in front of her hiding spot. She saw the fresh memory of Jay's beam grabbing the thing's image, lighting it up for just a second before his plasma stream crashed in among its set of multiple eyes. There was no time to count how many orbs it had or how many different ways they focused at once, but the thing already had its enormous maw open. Its mandibles had flexed wide to allow the round set of jagged fangs to come forward. It was ready to bite something, anything, what ever thing was nearest, posing the greatest threat.

Thank God for Jay.

"Mozart, you fool," she whispered. Strangely, she felt no tears sting her eyes. There were too many people to protect to fall victim to emotions at that moment. She had to stay strong. She had to lead. Like Electra would.

Chapter Fifteen

Morning eventually dawned, as morning always did. Even though cold had seeped into her bones until it seemed to hold them in one solid cramped mass of discomfort against the rocky seat she'd selected next to the cleft's opening, she knew it was time to get out and get her crew moving. She glanced back at Trane and Shayla asleep against either side of the sleeping dragon. Together, they would have kept the dragon warm that way. *Kind of them,* she thought. The old man lay curled in the fetal position just a meter or so from them, but upon squinting, she could see that he kept the dragon's tail warm by using it for a pillow. Or a long lost lover from his dreams of Christmastime on Earth. One of the two.

She looked back out the cleft to see Kor pulling Red from their hiding spot. A tickle of emotional discomfort played at the back of her mind. She wondered if he'd held her close to him to keep the injured tighter warm through the night. Then she wondered why that would be something to care one way or another about.

Slowly unfolding her legs to their complaints, Khiry stuck a hand out the cleft and waved. She wasn't sure if anyone would remember where her group had hidden, the way Jay had remembered. Remembered and defended.

The female transport saw Khiry do this and, from her hiding spot still shadowed by a taller hill, reached out her arm to wave as well. It was a promising sort of sign, Khiry decided. It was a sign of life and sustaining power. They'd made it through the night.

Khiry had pulled her hand back in through the brush and brambles to wake her companions. The female transport hadn't. Her happy voice accompanied her wave. "We made it in here!" Her triumphant shout ended with a scream that demanded Khiry's attention. She spun back to the slit of an opening to see something large and solid dragging the woman, brush, bramble, grass, and all, from the hiding spot by her arm. It was dragging with its unhinged mouth, gnawing through the flesh and into the bone of her arm as it pulled her out into the shadows of the hillside.

Kor had already let loose a shout and pulled his gun from his belt. It took only a second to spang the touched, to send its bits of bone and internal organs flying in a spray of red and fat. As if no one else screamed around the group, as if shock didn't set in among anyone else, Kor sprinted to the woman's side, shouting to the only other person left in her hiding spot. "Get out! Get out into the sun!"

Gibson sprinted out toward the light.

Kor dropped to the woman's side, yelling, "Hold on, Susha," and adjusted the setting on his gun. As smoothly as any surgeon, he pressed one hand against her shoulder and moved the weapon within inches of the socket. She screamed, "no!" But he had to do something. He had to try something and this was all he could think of. He cut cleanly with the weapon's stream through her arm, taking it off and cauterizing the wound in one shocking, excruciating moment. She passed out. He glanced around for any other threat while he scooped her up of the grass and ran with her to the sunny area where the others gathered.

"Let's get moving," he said to Khiry. She nodded. Onyx had unfolded himself from an outcropping of rocks where he blended spectacularly and sniffed at the injured human. He looked to Khiry as if questioning her.

"I'm not sure that you saved her," Khiry said.

"We'll see soon enough."

"You're going to carry her?" Gibson asked in disbelief. It was obvious he would prefer they leave the poor woman behind. No matter his "relations" with the woman in the night after Jay had sacrificed himself to the dark, Gibson had no loyalty to her. "What if she wakes and bites you?"

"Let's get moving while we have this discussion," Kor suggested.

"Agreed," Khiry said. "Are we all here?" She looked specifically for Shayla and then Red. "Do we have all our belongings? Food for the journey? We're moving fast today."

Gibson started moving in a northerly direction, but grumbled as he did so. "She'll wake and bite you before you can drop her and shoot her."

"Don't be such a whining tagger, Gibson," Trane said. "It's not you we've asked to carry her."

"And we can't just leave her," Khiry said sadly, thinking of Jay alone in the dark with the touched chasing him to his inevitable death.

Kor glanced at her. He breathed a little more heavily than normal now that he carried a full grown woman and moved at a brisk walk while doing so. "We're not leaving anyone. Anyone not with us right now is dead."

"I know that," she said.

"They're right," Bilal said to no one in particular, as if convincing himself. "We can't just leave her."

Electra jogged a few steps to catch up to the two of them, to join this conversation. "I've had many fine officers give their lives to protect me," she said. "To protect members of my family. What Jay did last night was noble and honorable. If you wish to have a ceremony of some kind in his name, I could lead something appropriate when we get to the city tonight."

Khiry felt a flush in her cheeks. "I'm sure Shayla would appreciate that."

"Shayla," Kor scoffed. "It's no secret he doted on *you*. He came to *your* rescue before those creatures could find your hiding place. I doubt Shayla factored into the act but as an afterthought. He saved you." He paused only a beat, but it was a beat that gave more emphasis to his words than he intended. "Before I could."

Khiry's flush deepened. "I think you see more than Mozart would have intended."

Kor gave her a sideways smile, not realizing that the one-armed woman he carried grew somehow heavier. Like a frog in heating water, he didn't notice the slow change. "Subtlety doesn't work on you, then?" he teased.

Electra gave a soft laugh and let her stride slow a bit. Soon the two walked alone ahead of the group. Alone except for a potentially dangerous creature in Kor's arms.

"I don't believe Mozart tried to be subtle or otherwise," Khiry said. "He was merely our computer tech. A good one at that. He'll be sorely missed when we get to the city."

Kor nodded, accepting that she'd missed his point. "We have others who are good with computers. Yourself. Bay. No doubt every one of the terraformers will be able to troubleshoot everything we need to get off this planet. I assume that's your worry? Getting home?"

She nodded. "Home."

The creature in his arms stirred ever so slightly.

"Hey, there! You guys left me!" a voice called jovially from the hills to their right.

* * * * *

Gibson wasn't waiting for someone to give him an order. He got down on one knee to line up his sight on the figure of Jay loping down the hillside toward them, swinging an oversized plasma streamer gun in one hand, a knife in the other.

When the whine of Gibson's gun started up, Trane knocked him off balance. "We'll see first," he hissed at the security chief sprawling in a cursing cloud of dust on the ground. It was the first Trane noticed the road had recovered from the previous day's soaking rain.

Bilal moved out ahead of the group, to intercept Jay, but the group followed. He'd get no privacy to interrogate the alien, to assess whether he posed a threat.

"Give us some distance," Bilal shouted.

Jay raised his arms as if in surrender. "There's no worry," he called back. "Come take my weapons so I can't harm anyone. Look how light I am." He stopped walking to bounce a bit in his boots. "No worries, mate!"

Kor looked at Khiry. "Where'd he learn that?"

She shrugged. "I'm sure we've transported Australians on the Instigator before."

"There's not so many of them left now that the continent's nearly gone," Kor muttered.

"Bigger worry right now," she said, pointing toward Jay.

Bilal had stopped walking, letting Jay close the distance then. Everyone watched the alien's stride, watched his easy smile. It certainly looked like Jay. Shayla said so to Khiry. The dragons rested quietly alongside the road, not concerned about the approaching person that they'd traveled with so far. Onyx seemed more concerned about the one in Kor's grasp, but no one noticed that at this point. All eyes were trained on Bilal and Jay. All ears strained to hear their conversation.

"How many touched did you bag last night?" Bilal asked.

"Truly? I lost track," Jay said, squinting into the sun. "I got the one in front of Khiry's hiding spot, and the inhabitant. Then I just started running for my life, spanging as I went."

"I assume you found somewhere to hide?"

"Yes. Just like our plan. A cleft in the rocks. I dove in praying to your god that there'd be no inhabitants or otherwise waiting inside for me. I was able to defend it because they couldn't get in. After a while, they seemed to give up. I think they were looking for another way in. Like Kor said before, they're smart. Organized."

"And you stayed hidden 'til sunrise?"

"It was a sound plan."

Because everyone strained to hear them, breathing as quietly as they could, they all heard the low, menacing growl come from Kor. Only it wasn't Kor who growled.

He shouted in surprise as the woman in his arms sprang to violent life. Of course he let go, but she had grabbed his neck with her remaining arm, grabbed his shoulder-length hair like a handle to pull his face toward her gaping maw. So while her legs fell heavily down the front and side of his body, she hung from his neck and head as if latching on to him like a vampire from Earth's mythology.

Gibson cursed, not out of worry for the warrior man's condition, but because he was missing a great opportunity to "accidentally" shoot the warrior man. Trane had knocked his gun loose and there was no recovering it now. At least, he couldn't recover it, pretend to shoot the touched, spang Kor instead, and expect that to look accidental while Trane and Bilal both had weapons already set on the creature.

Without thinking, Khiry grabbed the superstrong woman-beast by the shoulders, pulling for all she was worth. Electra was the next closest to them and dove in at the creature's legs, pulling her down.

"Get clear!" Trane yelled. "Get clear!" As Gibson had observed, he already had the creature in his weapon's sight, but the women fighting it were in danger. Too much motion and chaos didn't give him a clear shot. Kor wrenched his own head free of the demon's grasp and pulled Khiry's torso with one arm. His other arm grabbed at Electra, not getting a good purchase on her, but somehow rolling her free as he lost his balance and tumbled unceremoniously to his back in the dirt. The sound of the plasma streamer's fire whizzed through the air a second before the splatter of guts and blood. Electra made a gagging sound. Obviously, something gross fell on her.

Khiry dropped to her knees next to Kor, her heart lodged firmly in her throat and her stomach propped solidly right behind it. "Tell me she didn't bite you."

Kor struggled to sit up next to her, dust choking him as he spoke. "No, no, she didn't get a hold on me."

Others moved toward them then, relieved to see the woman-beast disintegrated. Trane held out a hand to Electra. Despite the dust and bits of guts, she remained regal and beautiful. From a near distance, the dragons watched in bored disinterest.

"Looked like her one good hand had a hold on you," Bilal mocked. "Good reason to cut that hair."

Electra gave the sarcastic man an appreciative glance. It took a strong person to lighten the mood after such a scene and she recognized that kind of strength when she saw it. She also recognized that he'd let Jay get closer to the group during the crisis. Apparently, Bilal was willing to admit when he was wrong.

"I knew she was affected," Gibson said to no one in particular. No one in particular listened to him.

"Smear it all, Kor, you scared the life out of us all," Khiry hissed through gritted teeth. She climbed to her feet already, tugging him to his feet as well. Beating the dust and dirt from his back, she continued a muttering, puttering tirade. "You could have ended up just like them. The last thing we need is to lose one of our strongest warriors. Just got Mozart back and you're dropping like one of 'em bit you." She stopped pummeling him to face him. "You're too kind-hearted for warrior work. Better to stick to being a marksman after this."

He bowed his head to her, a strange smile playing under his beard.

The others had watched this interaction with varying levels of interest, amusement, or wonder. Electra gave Trane a knowing smile. Just a few paces away then, Bilal shook his head. The terraformer looked back to Jay to finish his interrogation. The difference between Jay and the female transport had just become obvious. Questions were moot now. "So, Jay, how'd you survive the night out there alone?"

Jay winked at him and answered, "Just pretended I was Kor."

Electra couldn't help chuckling to herself. At least the alien had a realistic outlook about the situation.

"Kept asking myself, 'what would Kor do here?' And each time a touched came at me, I did what Kor would do to stay alive."

Jay received an amused smile from Khiry for his sarcasm, which was enough to keep him through the morning.

Chapter Sixteen

Walking at a brisk pace for eight hours taxed them all. Shayla finally complained of the cramps in her legs.

Khiry looked to Bilal. "Are we close?"

While Shayla was a full-grown woman, Khiry—and just about everyone else in the group—viewed her simple mindset and juvenile personality as childlike. The need to protect her was ingrained in most of them.

Despite that desire to protect, or perhaps because of it, Bilal shook his head. "Not close enough. We shouldn't stop unless we're making the decision to hide there for the night." He pointed at the foothills too far to their right.

Khiry squinted at the mountains and considered the upward trek to find hiding places. Her crew members were already tired. Their legs, unused to so much physical exertion, already turned to gelatin and twitching muscle under this torture and high heat. She wasn't sure they could climb right now. Asking them to walk further—and faster—was taxing enough.

"Can we eat these berries?" the old man called out.

Most of the group looked back at the man about thirty meters off the path.

"Don't move!" Bilal snapped. He looked to Khiry. "Can you get the dragons on the path? On the road?" He moved among the group toward the old man, saying, "Everyone stay on the road, now. We're closer to the city than I thought. We've made good time today. Stay off the grasses."

Khiry signaled to Onyx and motioned for him to get on the path. He followed her pointing finger with his gray-blue gaze. To her, he appeared bored. In truth, the regal beast just weighed his options. Walking on the grass was more comfortable for the heavy beasts than walking on packed dirt. He needed a reason to choose the more difficult option.

Bilal reached the edge of the road just opposite the old transport and looked across to him. The man stood next to one of a hundred or so clumps of bushes that speckled each hectare square area along the path. In his hand, he held up a branch of the nearest bush and the group could see it loaded down with chunky blue orbs gathered in bunches like cocktail grapes from Earth.

"Yes, those are edible," Bilal finally answered. "But we use them as a trap to lure the touched into the landmine area. You're in danger there. Can you retrace your steps exactly back to the road?"

The old man looked down at his feet, as if weighing the question. When he looked back at Bilal, he seemed to have aged ten years. Not an easy feat for his already wrinkled face and glassed-over eyes. "I think so. Let me go ahead and get these while I'm here."

"We've hardly time for that," Gibson muttered.

The curly-haired Shayla with her constant sweet disposition finally frowned at Gibson. Her mouth watered for the fruit the old man named Smith promised to bring back, but she understood that he did this at great danger to himself. Why would Gibson be short with the old man?

"Be careful, Smith," she called.

He smiled and waved to her before applying a pocketknife to his task. He had four berry-loaded branches in his arms when he started back, surveying the ground at his feet as if he could see the footprints he'd left in the grass a few moments before.

Electra closed her eyes and put a hand on Khiry's arm. "I can't watch."

"Shayla," Kor said. "Come help me with this backpack, would you?"

Of course Smith couldn't see footprints that no longer existed on the grass. He stepped cautiously, placing his boot down gently before applying his weight. One step at a time. Bilal motioned for the group to move on down the road toward the city, but stayed where he was, nodding to Smith. "Good step. Relax and try the next."

Khiry joined Kor in distracting Shayla when the explosion rocked the area. All hands jumped. Red screamed. Trane swore. The dragons grumbled and mumbled in their dragon speech, understanding now why Khiry had motioned them onto the dirt road. Onyx bowed his head to her. Once again, his favorite human had made him happy.

Blue clumps of berries rained down on their path like manna from Heaven, but none of them picked any up to eat. *There'll be no more talk of Christmastime on Earth,* Khiry thought sadly. She pursed her lips and looked straight ahead.

"At least we know what the landmines sound like now," Gibson said.

"Shut up," Jay warned him.

"What? I'm just saying that old man's death's not in vain. We've learned something from it. When the untouchables come for us in a couple hours, we'll know how close we are to death when we hear—"

Khiry turned to walk backward and lob an insult at the idiot, not sure if she was going to correct his name for the demons they ran from or merely tell him to shut up and guard the group's rear. She didn't get a chance to do either. Jay's lightning fast fist into the security chief's jaw silenced Gibson's heavy sarcasm.

"Thank you, Mozart," Khiry said. "I couldn't have done that better myself."

He smiled at her. "You could've used something more permanent like a radiator gun."

Gibson shook his head as he climbed up from the dirt path. The group already moved ahead without him. The young dragon looked over his shoulder at the human brushing dust from his clothes and gently touching his lower lip to check for blood. Bilal put a hand to the dragon's front claw to draw its attention back to the path.

"Radiator guns leave more broken bones under the skin," Electra said, pretending to misunderstand Jay's meaning. "Oh, you mean she could've shot him?" She winked one of her exotic eyes at Jay. "One of these days...he'll get his due."

"Maybe the berries will entice the touched to stop and meander among the mines," Kor suggested quietly.

Khiry sighed. "I'm searching for meaning in his death, too."

"Gibson has a point," Kor admitted. "Vile as it is."

"I know. I hadn't thought of it before, but we'll know when they're coming for us when they start blowing up. And we'll know what it sounds like." She paused while they walked a few paces. "I'll hear it in my sleep."

"Maybe the birds will eat the berries."

She glanced sideward at him. "That's a pleasant thought, but..."

"But?"

"I've not seen any birds on this horrid planet."

*   *   *   *   *

An hour had passed since Smith's demise and shadows reached for them from the mountains far to the right. As if providing paths for the touched, the shadows slowly stretched their lazy fingers toward the road where Khiry's people walked out in the open, out where dusk announced its intention to settle with a whisper of fog so close to the ocean to their left.

Khiry could swear she heard a howl somewhere inside the dimness of the shadows, a howl that sent a shiver up her spine. She looked nervously to Kor. He winked in a self-assured manner and took Shayla by the hand.

"You know some lovely Irish lullabies," he told the simple woman. "I bet your dragon friend would enjoy hearing one at the close of a long day of travel."

Her cat-like green eyes stared at him knowingly. For just a moment, he believed she knew that he intended to distract her. She smiled kindly and moved back through the group to Junior's side. The dragon seemed pleased for her company.

Khiry motioned for Bilal to join her at the front of the group.

"Where are the vehicles Rewk promised to send out? I can see the city on the horizon, but no one's coming out to help us. The sun's setting—"

"Something's definitely wrong," he said. "With the fog coming in off the ocean, they would be making preparations against condensation. It's worse here than on Earth. The conditions…well…no time for explaining. Even so, she should have people enough to send out drivers to collect us. This makes no sense."

"As you say, something must be wrong," Kor mused. "We need to pick up the pace."

"Everyone's already tired out," Khiry said. "I can tell we've slowed."

From the back of the group, Shayla's pretty voice drifted a haunting melody over them.

Over in Killarney
Many years ago,
Me mither sang a song to me
In tones so sweet and low.

"We need to impress upon them…" Khiry said.

"Might as well tell them the truth," Bilal said. "Can only help at this point."

She nodded.

"If the drivers haven't come out, the drawbridge is likely to be up," Bilal said. "We'll have to go in through a trap door."

Kor grimaced. "Just in case, you want to tell us where that is?"

The other man didn't smile. There was no humor in this. What Kor said made sense. They were likely to be attacked on the road. They were likely to lose more people. If Bilal was one they lost, the others would need to know how to get in the city.

Just a simple little ditty,
In her good ould Irish way,
And I'd give the world if she could sing
That song to me this day.

"To the east of the drawbridge, coastal side, away from the mountains," Bilal struggled to say. "Follow the stone wall, but stay extremely close to it. Within a meter and a half, no more than the height of a woman or you risk stepping on a landmine. Follow it to a point where it juts out in a V shape. At that V, there'll be a latch. The latch is a trick. Pull the latch and you'll lose an arm before all manner of rocks and boulders come tumbling down on you."

"Don't pull the latch," Khiry murmured as she walked.

"Directly down from the latch, at the ground, there are some stones that could be covered with grass and weeds now. The stones aren't obvious, but they're there. Clear them aside and you'll see a lever in the ground. Pull that up and the dirt will fall away as you lift up a door. There's a ladder that will let you into a city tunnel. The tunnel brings you up just beside the drawbridge."

"Latch on the ground, under the stones," Khiry muttered to herself. To Bilal she said, "Got it."

> *Oft in dreams I wander*
> *To that cot again,*
> *I feel her arms a-huggin' me*
> *As when she held me then.*

"I hope I'm at your side if we need to use it," Bilal said.

"I hope the same," Kor said.

"Such good planning in your defenses," Khiry said. "Why is something so simple as condensation thwarting us now? Wouldn't you know about the condensation before you built? Why would you select a place so close to the shore? I mean, given condensation problems? Given events on Earth?"

"Another time," Kor said. "You want to speed everyone up, or shall I?"

She nodded and turned to walk backward. "Everyone!" she shouted, interrupting the strange reverie they'd entered listening to Shayla's magical voice. "We've got to move faster. Dusk's coming on and our escort hasn't met us yet. We should jog. Jog as if your lives depend on it."

Red blanched. "God, save us," she said.

Electra grabbed the woman's one hand and put a spring in her own step. "Let's go. Ready? Jog with me." She got her going and released her hand to make it easier for running.

"We've got less than an hour before they attack," Gibson said to Trane. "We'll never make it."

"You'll have more air for running if you don't talk."

Chapter Seventeen

As Kor had said, the touched were intelligent and organized. They had learned over time that the grassy areas leading up to the city were dangerous. Lumbering across these areas often meant exploding death for the touched or a distracted inhabitant. So they kept to the dirt road that the colonists had used to get to the Uranium mine—the road that conveniently led straight to and from the inhabitants' lair.

Because the touched stayed to the road, Gibson's theory was flawed. They certainly knew when the first stupid touched ran off toward a clump of berry bushes. The group hesitated in jagged clumps of confusion when they heard the horrible yet familiar explosion. It rattled Red's nerves, but she didn't scream this time.

"They're coming now," Gibson muttered.

He was wrong. They'd already been coming. The creatures they feared had already been lumbering along the road behind them, ever since the shadows' fingers had silently slipped over its dirt path.

"Faster," Khiry shouted.

Her command was hardly necessary.

"The city is just ahead!" she called back to them. As Bilal had predicted, the drawbridge was up. She could see the monstrous wall looming ahead of them, its gray stone almost bleached white by the few seasons of sun it had already seen. The whiteness of it shone like a beacon, reflecting what daylight remained from the setting sun over the ocean to their left. The fog that gathered at their feet had slowly been thickening and stretching upward as if intending to meet the falling dusk halfway. The two events were in collusion against them. She wondered how they'd see the stones that hid the trap door into the city if the fog continued to thicken.

"We're almost there!" she called out. "Stay against the wall as we go around it. stay up against the wall! Don't step out onto the grass! Stay against the wall!"

She wasn't sure how many behind her listened, how many still followed, how many understood her commands. Weapons fire and screams answered as she bolted toward the drawbridge ahead. The idea of cutting across the grass toward the V in the wall tempted her greatly. She could see the goal. But thoughts of Smith blowing apart and his Christmas berries raining down on the path filled her mind. Stay on the road, she told herself.

"Khiry!" Shayla yelled.

Junior had taken to the sky, lifting Shayla up, up, up. She saw the girl go up over the wall. She nearly ran into the drawbridge with Kor right beside her. *Turn left.*

"Stay against the wall!" she yelled again, leading anyone still following in the fog and dusk toward the V in the wall.

Trying to hug the structure slowed her travel, but the sound of multiple explosions glued her to her purpose. She reached the V and dropped into the fog. She looked up for the latch, fixed it with her eyes, and brought her gaze down, straight down to the ground. The stones lay in a heap right where Bilal said they would.

"Faster!" Bilal yelled.

The sounds of plasma streamers whining directly overhead startled her into motion. She scraped her fingers and tore her nails on stones the size of her hands and forearms, flinging them off toward the grass. It occurred to her that some might hit mines. Those that did gave the touched reason to pause.

Another member of her group shouted for her to hurry. She saw the lever. *Success!* She grabbed it. Not all the stones were gone, but adrenaline gave her strength to move the whole wall if they needed that done. She hoisted the trap door up and open.

Rewk waited just beneath at the top of the ladder. Her contorted features and bulging eyes jumped out of the dark with a shriek. Khiry screamed as she fell back. Bilal turned as Rewk vaulted her solid, renewed weight out of the hole with superhuman strength. She fell on Bilal with a wail of the undead and the two rolled in a tangled mass of overweight muscle and teeth. Bilal's weapon fired off into the fog, missing the woman-beast on top of him, but such things didn't matter any longer. They rolled across a landmine and the explosion rocked the stunned crew.

With trembling hands, Khiry yanked her flashlight from her belt and shone it down the ladder. "Good enough. Let's go."

"Me first," Jay said. "*I'll* clear the way."

He dropped the distance without using the ladder's rungs. "Come on!" he shouted back to her.

Red, Gibson, Electra, and Trane clamored down next. "Go," Kor ordered her, firing at a touched beast just a few meters back.

Onyx flapped toward them.

"No!" she screamed. "Don't land!" She waved her arms in an X pattern, crossing them out in front of her, trying to warn him away. Instead of landing, the creature banked in close to the wall and grabbed her.

"Good enough," Kor muttered, disappearing into the ground. He pulled the trap door shut behind him.

When he landed on both feet next to Jay, the alien met his eyes in utter disbelief. "God, save me, she's not—"

The color had already drained from Jay's face. Electra
saw the alien's knees going weak. They were about to lose
him.

"No, no," Kor said quickly. "Onyx grabbed her. He's
taken her over the wall to safety. She's safer than any of us
right now. Probably with Shayla and the other dragons
already."

Jay's tangible relief made Gibson snarl. "Peggin'
mixers," he muttered.

He would never know how lucky he was that neither
man nor alien heard him.

* * * * *

Khiry closed her eyes at first, and then decided she
needed to know where they landed. She braced herself for
this new sensation. Onyx flapped his massive, strong wings
once to soar over the drawbridge, over a large ornate
fountain, over what seemed a commerce section of the city.
She noted that the place looked deserted. Nothing stirred
beneath them unless it was disturbed by the draft of the
dragon's powerful wings. Even then, it seemed only dust-
devil-like balls of debris and trash scattered across a vacant
street to a vacant building with vacant windows. Darkness
prevailed in this city beneath her. Infrequent cones of
bluish light cast minimal pools of hope, but, overall,
something that came to feed in the gloaming had
extinguished life and light in this place.

Onyx slowed to a sort of descent near a central-looking
structure amid this apocalyptic grayness. It wasn't really in
the center of the city. Far from it. The city was too large for
them to reach the center that quickly. It was a too-large
expanse of tall, deathly quiet buildings. The building Onyx

landed next to with his bulk creating an almost ripple in the asphalt pavement was a large, round, civic-center type of building. He flexed his muscular hind legs to take the impact of the landing and set her down on her feet. It seemed incongruous in this place of desertion. Why a civic center? Why a place of gathering?

She stood with her arms outstretched for a moment, getting her bearings. No, the ground didn't tilt. With an uneasy smile, she looked up at her dragon's gray-blue eyes. "Thank you, my friend. You've saved my life."

He bowed his head as if acknowledging what she said. She was pretty sure he didn't understand her words, but surely he understood the meaning. Hopefully. How else did you thank a dragon for saving your life? These were wild, alien creatures. She wasn't sure if it was because adrenaline still pumped through her body or because she was so grateful to be alive, but she moved the few steps to him and placed her arms as far around his huge belly as they could reach. With a flashlight still gripped in one hand and a plasma gun in the other, this seemed inappropriate, somehow fake. She rested her head against the giant creature's belly for a moment. This excuse for a hug would have to convey what she couldn't say with words.

Shayla's voice interrupted her.

"Oh, Khiry! You made it!"

"You must be Rewk's dragon leader," a man said.

Khiry turned from Onyx to face a muscular scientist. She found that bizarre. First, she had to recover from the shock of seeing someone alive in this dismal place. Then, she had to put aside her stereotypes. Given the colonists' predicament, more than security officers would have to bulk up and learn how to fight for survival. The dirt-streaked lab coat with its rolled sleeves and carefully embroidered name "Timo" on the breast made her assume this short, muscled man with the too-short hair cut was a scientist. That and the thick-framed glasses hanging from a chain around his neck.

"Let me take you somewhere safer."

Khiry looked down at Shayla. "Where's Junior?"

"There's food in the civic center. He'll come along with T-Rex soon enough. Did you know they can find us by scent?"

Khiry couldn't find it in herself to smile, and wondered where Shayla had learned something like that. Maybe this scientist had suggested it to her. Out of the corner of her eye, she thought she saw another dingy lab coat disappear behind a stone column of the civic center. But it moved too quickly. It had to be her imagination. This place couldn't have two survivors.

Chapter Eighteen

"This place was supposed to be beautiful," Shayla breathed, almost dreamily, almost sadly. Khiry looked down at her, wondering how much she really understood about the terraformers' purpose. When she followed Shayla's gaze to a lamp post not two hundred meters ahead of them, she thought she understood.

Something as simple as a lamp post had been given enormous attention. Someone had carved it from hard, heavy stone. Its base was, as it should be, wider than the top it sloped toward, but the top branched to extend into what seemed like an ornate arm of curlicues and ivy leaves to hold the carved stone lamp that now emitted a crisp, bluish sort of light. LED lamps would, of course, be easier to power. But why was this lamp the only one standing? A colony that gave so much attention to placing something as simple as a lamp post should have them standing every…

Her thoughts trailed as her eyes followed the once-smooth asphalt street. Of course there were more. And each was as lovely as the first. But each was down in various states of brokenness or shattered mess. Lamps destroyed and light doused. Something large and heavy and destructive had barreled through this street, cracking the perfect pavement with huge, wide strides and knocking not just lamp posts, but also windows and bits of once-strong buildings out of place.

She looked at Timo, the scientist, who frowned deeply.

"No inhabitant or touched has ever done something like this," he murmured. "Not even a group of them could do so much damage." He looked at her directly. "And *why* would they, we wondered. Their purpose is to feed. Not to destroy. This is unnatural to them."

"Maybe we've introduced something new," Khiry whispered more to herself than to either Shayla or their guide. "We haven't seen a living soul yet." She stopped herself before she said aloud "including our other dragon friends."

Timo nodded. "There's been a lot of activity since your ship landed. Some of us thought the touched and the inhabitants might have been stirred up by the prospect of new blood. A lot of us prepared to go underground, but…"

His voice trailed as he stared off toward a tower a few blocks away.

"But what?" she prompted.

"Something happened last night. When Rewk returned. She told us that we'd need to get the other two buggies out to go after your party. But an organized team of inhabitants attacked at dusk. Not touched, but inhabitants. They came in waves. I've never seen so many. They've destroyed almost every living thing. I lost track of how many I saw turned to the touched before dawn."

Khiry gasped. "What? How many people live here?"

"So many…so many missing…I think they came for the dragon."

The implication sent a shiver up her spine. She glanced again at the ornate buildings, once pre-fabricated victories over the barren planet, now demolished or dented ruins. A touched dragon could certainly do this.

"Timo, this is important. How many people are missing? How many people live in this city?"

"We have twelve hundred terraformers."

Her stomach turned at the implications. Twelve hundred touched loose in the city tonight? Unless the drawbridge had been raised after they'd sought the mountains at dawn. How lucky would that be? If the touched were still in the city, wouldn't they be upon this little group already?

"That includes farmers that have come in from the outlying farms in the past year or so," Timo continued. "When we realized we couldn't protect them from the inhabitants and the touched, we brought in the farmers and their families."

"Smear it all, Timo. Why didn't you call for help? Why haven't you gotten on one of your ships and left the planet?"

"We don't have the power for that. Our communications are down. It's one of the first things we lost."

She sighed. It's what Bilal and Rewk had explained. Of course they'd tried to get word out to Earth, but no one had responded. No one had come. The United Society for Peace and Strength was too busy dumping humans off the home planet in an effort to save Earth from Mankind's industrial warming effects. Bringing stray humans back wasn't on the agenda. Checking planets for dangers before sending humans there obviously wasn't part of the terraforming agenda, either.

"We've been using all our power for weapons and defense. We were praying your ship would have something…When she saw the wreckage, Rewk was devastated. She told us so yesterday. But she knew her men had to drive on and save you if they could. Get you back here to the safety of the city, even if it meant draining more power."

"This is madness. They've overrun your city and you've no way to get help?"

"We need new power coils, new nuclear reactors, new water tanks, everything. We can't do anything. We're sitting ducks."

Khiry recognized the note of hysteria somewhere beneath his despair. "We're not sitting ducks," she said.

"You didn't see the attack last night," he murmured. "We were locked in here with so much death."

She frowned. Maybe the drawbridge hadn't been lowered to let the twelve hundred touched of the city out. "My team is here now," she heard herself say to comfort him. "The dragons are here and they have strength and abilities we're hardly aware of. All we have to do is get the power coils from the Instigator and use them to communicate with Eldora Moon instead of powering some drawbridge or plasma canon or whatever you've been using them for."

"But we have to defend the city," he whined.

"Unless I'm mistaken, Timo, there's no city left to defend."

He stared at her in shock. Her words were brutal, but true. It was time to switch from the defensive mode he'd participated in the past dozen years to a plan for getting off the planet. He nodded, gulping back fear in the presence of this woman who had courage in spades. "Is it true you have Electra Endh with you?" he asked.

"Yes. She'll be pleased to have you on our team."

The man smiled as if placating her, instead of the other way around. It was an uncomfortable smile, but at least it wasn't the hint of hysteria she'd seen in him a few moments before. She thought he acknowledged hope now.

"Should we move faster?" Khiry asked him next.

"What do you mean?"

"If a thousand or so people have become touched within the city, and it's definitely dark here now, shouldn't we move faster to find shelter?"

He shook his head. "I've baited them."

"Baited them? What do you mean?"

Timo glanced up at Onyx. "The civic center has a retractable roof. It was open when Shayla came through with her young dragon friend and the larger one. I didn't realize there was another."

A strange feeling slammed Khiry in the gut. She hid her worry from Shayla and Timo, but Onyx sensed it.

"Can your dragon friend understand our words?"

Whether he could or not, Khiry answered, "No."

"Good. You see, I—"

She had a pretty good idea of what he was about to say. And she knew what she'd do to him as soon as he admitted it. So she interrupted him to ask two very important questions first. "Wait, is that tower the communications center?"

He followed her pointing finger with his gaze.

"Yes. The center is beneath the tower. But we haven't even tried to access the technology for years."

"I can imagine," she said. "A waste of time when you need to defend yourselves. Is that also where you keep the buggies?"

"Oh, no. Too far from the city entrance. Those are by the drawbridge. By the city fountain."

"That makes sense," she said, as if absorbed in the conversation, as if her brain wasn't roiling with the anger and worry rising inside her. "So you're sure the buggies are safe from the touched getting hold of them."

"I told you, I baited them," he repeated. "They're all drawn to the civic center now. There's no question. Even the inhabitants will go there."

"Because you trapped the dragons there."

Shayla gasped, but Khiry put her hand out to stop the little woman from getting hysterical.

"I'm a scientist. I have an aerosol I've been working on for years. I'll release it into the air ducts once all the touched are there and feeding."

"Once they're all there? What makes you think you can get them all there at the same time?"

"It's just a matter of time. The doors seal behind them like a mousetrap. More can get in, but nothing can get out. You're perfectly safe. I'll get you to shelter and go back to release—"

She'd heard enough. With a swift tilt and kick, she slammed her boot up into his face, sending him reeling. Her intent was to knock him out so she could go on without him.

Onyx hadn't understood the man's words, but he understood her action. He reached down with one powerful front claw and impaled the man on the pavement. Blood spurted from the wound and from Timo's mouth in matching founts.

"Back the way we came," Khiry hissed, turning on her heel. Something within her wept for the poor man bleeding out on the asphalt behind them.

*   *   *   *   *

They were only a city block from the civic center. They hadn't walked far at all. She stopped to secret Shayla in a dark doorway. Khiry took a plasma gun from her belt. "You know how to use this?"

"Kor showed me," Shayla whispered.

Khiry powered it up so its whine sounded faintly in the quiet city. She wasn't sure what to tell Shayla. Shoot anything that comes out of the building? What if Junior came out? Their eyes met. What if Junior came out touched?

"Don't run up to any of the dragons until you know they're safe."

Shayla nodded, tears brimming in her cat-like eyes.

Khiry looked up at Onyx next. "You're not going to like this."

She wondered what emboldened her to rush into an auditorium to rescue a set of dragons that might or might not already be dead from a horde of demonesque creatures. Maybe having Onyx at her side made the task seem easier? Or maybe she'd seen so much horror the past two days that one last quest before death appealed to her. Some great and honorable quest like this.

Khiry grabbed up a chunk of stone from a fallen lamp post on her way up the steps to the civic center doors. If the doors sealed behind her, she'd be just as trapped as the touched and inhabitants inside. Hopefully something as simple as a wedge could counter the "seal." She held the door open wide so Onyx could squeeze in—a tight fit—and then placed the stone upright to give the door the appearance of being closed.

They made their way as quietly as possible toward what Khiry hoped was a balcony that would overlook the central auditorium. Quiet, when walking next to a hulking dragon, was a relative term. His claws clicked on the marble-like flooring with each lumbering, waddling step of his massive hind legs. The effect was magnified by the fact that he leaned over slightly to keep from snagging his wingtips on the sprinkler system above.

The sprinkler system, she thought. The memory of Rewk pursing her lips as she said she'd recently learned that the touched could be killed by drowning rushed back to Khiry.

Well, every little thing helped. She tapped Onyx's front arm, motioning him toward a large opening that led to rows upon rows of seats overlooking the chaos of an arena full of terror below. Sure enough, her dragon companion growled at sudden understanding of their mission.

T-Rex and Junior huddled together in a cage with no roof in the middle of the auditorium. The cage itself was quite large, offering meter upon meter of empty space between them and the cage bars, between them and the hordes of touched who reached with bleeding, ugly hands for the free meal within. It was just a matter of time before they figured out how to climb the slippery vertical bars.

In one part of her mind, Khiry wondered why the colonists had this type of cage on hand. Timo couldn't have erected it in one day since Rewk's revelations last night, even if he had assembled the plan in that time.

The rest of her mind worked overtime on her own plan. She motioned to Onyx, showing him a cone of air from her mouth, expanding and reaching toward the ceiling where the sprinkler system sat waiting…waiting.

Onyx watched her with his wise gray-blue eyes for a moment. He thought he understood. Fire. It might kill them, but he was willing to try her plan because she was his trusted human. She was here at his side to rescue his friends from a cage for the second time. He reared his head back and loosed a stream of hot red-orange flame at the ceiling far above the wailing cacophony. When he stopped with no result, she encouraged him to do it again. Smoke filled the space in the top of the auditorium and beasts began crawling toward them.

A dragon was difficult to hide when he started spewing flame.

This time, Onyx's cloud of fire succeeded. An alarm began to ring, shrill and all around them. Water burst forth in a chaotic spray from every sprinkler in the building. Sealed as the building was against an aerosol getting out, she had no doubt the water would begin to collect in no time.

Onyx looked down at the touched climbing toward them and loosed another cloud of fire. Despite the water causing most to slip and fall, the fire caught on their clothes and loose skin. Screams of terror joined their wails of anger and hunger.

Onyx saw that Khiry had her weapon drawn and powered for a fight, and he lifted off from the balcony. He swooped down to his friends, banging the cage over to empty them out the side. As Junior jumped out, Onyx grabbed the young one in his claws and lifted off again. T-Rex rose into the air and soon the touched were jumping, trying to grab their escaping meal.

"Too easy," Khiry muttered as the three joined her on the balcony. Onyx nudged her with his regal head to move her toward the doorway they'd come in.

Running for their lives, the four made for the door she had propped open. In the hall ahead, she saw a lab coat flutter around a corner. "Smear it all," she shouted. "Onyx, go! Go!"

She motioned him toward the door with the stone. He understood her, but didn't understand why she ran ahead, calling out words he couldn't speak.

"Hello!" she yelled. "You've got to get out of here, whoever you are! Come on! Follow me!"

As she rounded the corner where she'd seen the lab coat flutter, she saw a man bent over a panel on a door. It was obvious he worked frantically to punch in some code to let him through the door.

"Come on, mister," she said. "There are touched and inhabitants down in the auditorium. I'm drowning them. We've got to go before they figure out how to get up here."

The man replied while he punched numbers. "I have to make sure this plan doesn't fail. I have a toxin to release."

"I've broken the seal on this place. Let's get out."

He threw an annoyed look at her. "I'm sure those you're with have closed the door behind them. You're with me now. Come on. The touched can't get in here."

With a click, the lock turned over and the door swung open.

Chapter Nineteen

Kor led the small team down the tunnel toward what he knew was the drawbridge. If Gibson had been paying attention, he'd know that was the logical direction they traveled. It took no time to reach another ladder and the group made a cautious exit to the open and dark city.

"Found the other buggies," Trane said.

"Makes sense," Kor said. "Near the city's entrance."

"We should figure out how to lower the drawbridge," Gibson suggested. "Get in the buggies and go after the power coils. We use those to get their ships up and running. We get off this rock."

Kor looked back at him as if he were crazy, not dignifying the suggestion with an answer.

"Lower the drawbridge?" Trane asked. "Right now? While those creatures are out there?"

"Those buggies can outrun any one of those untouchables," Gibson barked.

"Those buggies are solar powered, you melon," Trane told him. "Shut up until you have something constructive to offer."

Gibson scowled as he turned to follow Kor and found himself bumping directly into Jay. "Just content to leave Shayla and Khiry to fend for themselves in the city?" Jay asked him. "Some security chief you are."

"You heard Kor. They're with the dragons. They're safer than we are."

* * * * *

Khiry sat at a computer control panel so much more sophisticated than the one on the Instigator. Before her, a monitor spit out data and digits that made no sense to her brain. Beyond that, a window to the auditorium showed the chaos of touched trampling each other in their fear of the rising water. It certainly wasn't enough to drown anyone on its own, but if you held someone down, if you stepped on someone weaker than yourself…

"Khiry Okerson," the scientist named Lenny said. "Type in the code I gave you. It's time."

She swallowed hard against a lump that had formed in her throat. She had unwillingly joined this man in his suicide mission to save a foreign planet. Oh, sure, there were probably more touched "out there." Of course there were more inhabitants in the mountains. But this group here, this mass of teeming death squads would be annihilated and her people would be safe for the rest of the night.

"The good of the many outweighs the good of the one," she murmured.

Somehow, he heard her over the screech of the fire alarm.

"You don't have to preach utilitarianism to me, Miss Okerson. I do this to protect my family, my colony. There's no personal gain in dying with someone else's research in my lungs."

"Timo's."

"Yes. A sick bastard, but smart nonetheless. This will work. And it will be painless. Would you like to give me your hand?"

She smiled slightly. "Ah, the measure of a man. How we meet death."

"Indeed. I've typed in my code. There's only yours—"

What use did a person have for codes when they carried a plasma streamer gun? Kor blasted through the locking panel and the door that secured them in the little control room with a look on his face that suggested few people were going to survive his wrath. The sprinkler system had put a sheen on his muscles that highlighted his strength, as if Lenny would have doubted it after that entrance.

He tossed a menacing glare at the scientist and reached out his free hand to Khiry. Pulling her out of the chair and toward the door, he said to the man sitting in stunned silence: "Give us two minutes to get out if you're still bent on killing yourself."

He let the door slam behind him, but it could no longer click locked. It didn't matter. The touched wouldn't get up to the control room before Lenny sent the aerosol through the ducts.

"How did you find me?" she asked as they darted for the main door.

Shayla waited, holding the door open wide, and then pulled the stone from the doorway and let the door seal closed once they ran through. It didn't just click. It made a sort of suckling sound.

"I told him where the control room is," a woman said.

Khiry made a mental note that this one didn't look suicidal, but still had the worrisome lab coat over her blue jeans and t-shirt. "Ferra" was embroidered in black next to the coat's right lapel. *Black?* Khiry thought. *Isn't that the color for doctors, not lab rats?*

"I told him about the mad scientist," Shayla said.

Junior nuzzled Shayla as if the young woman was forgetting some solemn duty. She absently returned to stroking the dragon's jaw while they spoke.

"We should find shelter," Khiry said. "I believe there's a scientist in there killing off all the current touched from the city, but, I don't know exactly how they can be sure they have them all. And I *know* they don't have all the inhabitants from the area."

Ferra the doctor nodded. "I'm not sure how Timo's plan formed, but he seemed certain earlier today that he'd get all the touched to assemble at the auditorium."

"He tried to sacrifice our dragon companions," Khiry said.

The woman colored under the accusation in Khiry's voice and the color in the moonlight gave her a lovely glow. She was a pretty young woman; hardly old enough to be a doctor. "I—I didn't know. I'm sorry it came to that. I'm sorry he tried something so…" As if she realized how small her apology seemed, she stopped. "Let's get you to shelter. There are a few of us untouched and…well…pleasant company. We can let you rest after the ordeals you've been through."

At the base of the steps, Gibson watched the plan forming. He looked at Trane. "You're content to let them plan our future?"

"They've kept us alive this far, you melon. What's wrong with you?"

"I just think maybe we should be more careful about these terraformers. We don't know this woman—"

Ferra had colored again as she and the little group approached Gibson and his not-so-quiet tirade.

"This is Gibson, our *former* security chief," Khiry said. "He's an idiot. If you've got a shed or public bathroom to put him in for the night, that will serve us fine."

Ferra didn't laugh, but it was obvious the joke set her more at ease. "Your security chief has nothing to worry about from me."

"*Former* security chief," Kor corrected.

"I'm a doctor. I used to be a pediatrician, but…but now I treat anyone."

Khiry nodded at that. There were likely a great many injuries and illnesses in a colony beset by demons. So this Ferra was a young doctor. Her dark hair and smooth skin made her look no older than Khiry herself.

She must have been very young when she came to Eldora Prime. Had there been a school here? With children who grew up to become pediatricians and scientists and who knew what else? In the midst of abandoned buildings with broken windows and scarred walls, it seemed improbable that this city had ever had children walking its sidewalks, eating candy treats, carrying textcards of homework around or studying socialization after a long week of home-schooling.

"I'll take you to June Mill's house. It's big with many rooms. She had planned to make it into a sort of hotel for travelers from other cities as our terraforming progressed." The sadness in her voice told them she'd shared somehow in the woman's failed dream. "She's a lovely woman who'll welcome you and make sure you're well fed. And her husband knows how to keep the touched out of their place."

Chapter Twenty

The room Khiry sat in was as dark as any she'd been in so far. She used her trusty LED flashlight to provide enough light to get the simple bedside lamp turned on. Its yellow glow belied the power the colony was supposed to use. She still felt somehow comforted by the bluish glow from the flashlight. Maybe she'd keep both on for the remainder of the night.

The cot that would serve as her bed with its simple twenty-centimeter mattress felt like a luxury she shouldn't indulge in. If she slept too soundly, surely something would creep in and feed on her. And then there was the guilt.

She saw faces each time she closed her eyes. While showering in one of the home's luxurious recycled water rooms, she had closed her eyes to shampoo her hair. It shouldn't have taken much time, considering her hair only reached her shoulders, but the cleansing water felt as if it washed not just grime away, but also the stink of death. Unfortunately, as the pretty scents of flowers and clean soaps seeped into her hair and skin, the horrid images of the dead seeped into her head. They crept behind her eyes where she couldn't get at them, where she couldn't scrub them with her fingers or the cloth June Mill had given her. She could rub her face raw and the images of Jack on fire, Maas in the air, Susha being dragged into the open shadows of morning still played on the insides of her eyelids. She stood quietly sobbing in the shower, trying to keep her eyes open.

Now while she sat on the edge of her cot thinking about how to sleep with her eyes open, she felt the pull of nightmares tugging her toward sleep. This was going to be a long night.

The kindly June Mill, nicknamed Pesto by the colonists, had given her a blanket, but there were no sheets to spare tonight. "Come back tomorrow," June had said with a wink. "We'll round up all kinds of supplies from the empty homes. Prob'ly find us a new homestead if we can get past the ghosts."

Her husband had shushed her. "These are our neighbors you're joking about," he'd reprimanded her.

"Oh, and they wouldn't say the same about us to lighten the mood? Every one of us is ready to faint from the stress—"

"Just get everyone somewhere to rest," he'd argued. "No more lightening the mood at our neighbors' expense."

June had winked at Khiry, which Khiry thought was in very poor taste. Even before she started having visions of the recent "taken," of Rewk erupting out of the trap tunnel beneath the city wall, Khiry hadn't liked the idea of mocking the dead. She didn't like the way Mr. Mill spoke to his aging wife, but she also didn't like the woman's cavalier manner. Pesto spoke of scavenging off the dead. Electra had given her a kind but sad smile. This was part of leading. Not everyone reacted as a leader might want them to when a crisis hit.

In the quiet of the tiny compartment with her tiny cot and two tiny lights, Khiry thought about her leadership so far. She'd lost a lot of people on her way to Touch Down City. How much more death would morning bring? The hesitant knock on her door made her wonder if death had started early. Part of her welcomed the opportunity to go fight something instead of sleeping and dreaming.

"Come in," she said.

Kor nudged the door open and peered in. "I've come to watch over you."

She didn't try to hide her surprise.

"I've brought a whetstone to sharpen your bowie knife." He held up the tool he mentioned and her eyes brightened instantly. He took that as his invitation to stay, and stepped into the room, clicking the door closed behind him.

"I also want to ask you about Gibson."

"Ah, the real reason for your offering," Khiry said, taking the whetstone from him. He didn't correct her. Yet. He didn't tell her that her subtle scent of flowers and clean linens filled this little room to an intoxicating level.

She pulled the knife from her boot and placed its tip gently against the heavy brick in her hand. She glanced at him. "What of Gibson? I thought it would be Trane asking to fire him out an airlock first chance we get."

Kor didn't smile. He sat on the cot next to her and watched her work the blade. "We may still need him for defense. But I'm concerned about his interest in these power coils. And the Uranium stockpiled here. Did you notice how he got Mr. Mill off alone as soon as he could once he learned the man mined Uranium?"

"I noticed they went off alone, but I don't know what they went off to talk about. I was more concerned that these people have Uranium-235 stashed around. Not safe. And shouldn't they have been using it to get off the planet? Not storing it for a rainy day." She considered this a moment while she moved the stone against the knife. "I guess it'll be to our advantage if we can lift off using it to fuel their reactors. But what can Gibson want with Uranium? He's not smart enough to build a bomb."

"No, but he knows engines. He knows his way around a transport vessel, which these people have here."

She lowered the knife and stone a moment, considering this. "You think he'd make some kind of deal to get their ship running without telling us? Seems strange."

"Yeah, it does. But he's a tagger, and God only knows what he's hiding back on the Instigator. I don't for a minute believe he was sending us all to Pangaea for a holiday."

"Agreed," she murmured. "So we need to search the ship while we're there tomorrow. See what it is he's hiding."

"Then use it as leverage."

"Or go ahead and fire him out an airlock," she teased.

He liked that and spent the next few minutes watching her sharpen the knife in silence.

"Tell me why you joined the Instigator's crew," he finally said.

She glanced at him as if this was forbidden territory, then looked back to her work. "It's not been so long ago. Don't you remember?"

"Two years, I think. What were you? Fifteen?"

"Just that. My family went one way. I went another."

Nothing but their breathing and the metallic schick of the blade against stone filled the little room for a few minutes. "Had your family trained you to fly?"

She smirked. "Prodding?"

"Yes."

She held up her knife to examine its edge. It met her satisfaction. Wiping it against her pantsleg, she said, "My father taught me to fly a cargo ship we ran between Earth and the moon; Earth and Mars. Short runs to get supplies to the docks. He'd teach me longer jumps and how to get into hyperdrive when we didn't have jobs to do. I didn't know he was grooming me for a post in the resistance. It was a post I didn't want because I believed in what USPS could do to help Earth. I believed they were terraforming for a good cause. When my father revealed his plan to join the resistance, I went looking for employment with an honest crew."

"And you figured Marlon was honest?"

"Honest enough. And willing to hire someone my age. He transported people and legal cargo. At least he used to. But now here we are on a planet where USPS dropped off terraformers and stopped communicating with them when they found trouble. And it looks like the communication stopped merely to cover up a planning oversight. How irresponsible is that? Do these people deserve to live in fear and die because some scientists didn't do enough research and now a government doesn't want to look bad for it?"

"No. But you made the right decision two years ago. You couldn't join the resistance when you believed it was wrong."

"And I can't turn a blind eye to the horror here…"

He nodded. They were doing the right thing by helping the remaining terraformers of Eldora Prime get off the planet.

She returned her knife to her boot and placed the whetstone in the floor at the foot of the cot. "I'm ready to fall asleep now," she said. "You can return to your quarters."

"Direct."

"There's no point in us wasting words when we could be getting some much-needed sleep, Kor. You look about as worn out as I feel."

"There's something every warrior wants to hear," he muttered as he moved over on the cot. He propped the pillow in the corner behind him and leaned back into it. "I told you I'd come to watch over you. That's my intention. You've endured too much the past few days to sleep alone in this room with your nightmares waiting at the door."

She didn't smile. "How did you know?"

"Because these visions haunt me, too." He waited a moment for her to toss that about in her mind. Then he said, "Come here and let me hold you while you sleep."

She stared at him a moment.

"Was that too subtle?" he teased, the light reflecting off the pools of his chocolate brown eyes in some amused play.

"Why, I—I just don't think I need the marksman from the ship to hold—"

"I'm not the marksman from the ship. I'm the man who's made it his mission to see you safe and sound. Now lay your head on me." He held his arms out to her, pulling her into a warm embrace that she hadn't realized she craved.

What a lovely experience. What a wonderful feeling. As she closed her eyes, losing herself in the beating of his heart beneath her cheek, she pretended not to notice him positioning the plasma streamer canon on the table next to the tiny lamp. Within easy reach. Already pointed at the door.

Chapter Twenty-One

June woke them for an early breakfast and avoided losing her life by announcing herself before opening the door to Khiry's room. By the time Khiry, Kor, Red, Shayla, Gibson, Jay, Trane, and Electra were at the cozy wooden table in June's oversized kitchen, Mr. Mill had already made the excuse of going out to look for neighbors who needed help, and one neighbor had arrived to see the visitors. Seeing dragons outside June's house at sunrise had put the woman, whose name was Bev, in the mood for gossiping. She'd found no one else to gossip with because no one else in their sector of the city remained alive.

"I feel as if I'm on display," Gibson said to the buxom Bev. She giggled and flashed him a flirtatious smile over the flowered porcelain dishes. Either she'd come to Eldora Prime alone or she'd recovered from the loss of a partner easily. Khiry noted that with a freshly scrubbed body and coveralls borrowed from Mr. Mill, Gibson looked downright personable to this flirtatious Bev. She wondered for a moment if she was a tighter. Would terraformers bring tighters to a new planet? The doctor, Ferra, who'd brought them to this bed-and-breakfast-like home the night before also looked at Gibson as if seeing a different person in him.

Ferra looked at Kor as if studying him next. "You've cleaned up, Mr. McCormick, but your demeanor hasn't changed. You're very serious."

As if belying her observation, he lifted one of the flowery teacups to his mouth and swallowed some strong coffee. He had no idea it was the last of the coffee stores the colonists had and they'd been saving it for the past two years. He nodded in Ferra's direction. "We've had some serious trials the past few days."

The statement would have caused a more attuned man to sit down and shut up, but Gibson had something jolly in his mind that morning. He'd gotten out of a long-term relationship with the female transport he'd pagged while hiding in the foothills thanks to a stroke of luck. He'd likely get out of a long-term relationship with Red because she was still messed up in the head since her accident, despite her performance in his bed the night before. He imagined how easy it would be to get out of a commitment to a terraformer on a doomed planet while casting lusty gazes on Bev. He fantasized about the millions of dollars coming his way if he could get his special cargo off Eldora Prime. He gave no more thought to the people who'd died so far. Who could hold such dreary thoughts when the early morning sun was rising on so fine a house with its lacy curtains and yellow wallpaper? This home away from home was the perfect place to plan a mutiny.

As if mutiny were the subject in everyone's mind, Jay stood up from his place at the overly-friendly table and announced: "I don't think we *all* need to go to the ship. Doesn't seem there's any reason to put the ladies at risk when all we need is three drivers. There and back in a few hours, right?"

Kor raised his eyebrows in surprise. While he agreed with Jay's assessment, he was surprised the alien would stick his neck out for a strike from Khiry's feminist ideals. She bristled, of course.

"Shayla and Red will stay here where they're safe," Khiry said. "And Electra is her own woman. She has no need to journey out in the open. No one will question her for staying behind to guard our comrades."

Electra gave a light laugh at Khiry's choice of words. "To guard them," she murmured. "How quaint."

Khiry didn't stop to comment. "I'll go along because I'm responsible for your safety while you're under my leadership."

Jay snorted. "Then I relinquish you of your title. Kor, I'm under your leadership for the day."

Khiry's jaw fell open.

Kor chuckled.

"Afraid I have to second that motion for at least the morning," Trane said. "Kor, Captain, Leader. Are we ready to head out?"

Kor looked at Khiry. "I just have one order to give our second in command here."

She fumed.

"Stay here."

She fumed more.

Then he leaned close and whispered, "and keep an eye on Gibson."

"That's hardly fair," she muttered.

"No, but it's necessary. Do you think one of your dragons would come with us?"

She folded her arms across her chest and leaned back in her chair, looking off toward the window. "You don't deserve one of my dragons."

*　*　*　*　*

They were several kilometers from the city before any of them spoke. The whirring of the buggy had been their only company so far. Trane kept an eye off in the distance behind them for anything resembling a storm cloud. All he saw was Onyx flying circles around the city, performing routine sweeps for danger. T-Rex had flown ahead to the wrecked ship to wait for them, again, sweeping for danger. Kor figured Trane's voice tracking a storm or a frantic dragon bearing bad news would be the first he'd hear. Instead, Jay leaned forward to the driver's bench and asked, "So what did you tell her that made her agree to stay behind?"

Kor felt a half smile form beneath his beard. "I asked her to keep an eye on Gibson."

Jay nodded at that. "Wise. He's up to something."

"Had a fit when we said we were going without him," Trane offered from his place at the back of the buggy.

"We think he's got something hidden on the ship that he doesn't want us knowing about. Something he wants to sneak to Pangaea."

"Power coils," Jay said.

"What makes you think that?"

"Electra told me."

"How would she know?" Kor asked.

"It's the only thing that makes sense to her. She found them while she was sneaking about being a stowaway. Since he wasn't in on the captain hiding the dragons, she figures he must be the one who hid the power coils. She told me where to find them. Front compartments leading into the mess hall."

Kor glanced sideward at the alien. "You're not half bad as a spy."

Jay sat back in his seat. "I do what I can."

"Spy or not, I want to know how you got this information out of that USPS officer," Trane said. His tone suggested lechery.

"Now that's not for a gentleman to say."

Kor joined Trane in laughing. Both men knew what *that* meant. "Never pictured that pretty lady to betray her brother with a mixed relationship," Kor said. "I don't mean that in a prejudice way, either. I just mean, she's got family to answer to. You fancy yourself taken with her?"

"Naw, not in love. The gal I'm in love with has eyes for someone else right now."

"Oh, now my dog ain't in that fight," Trane said. "I'll just step out of the conversation at this point."

Jay shook his head, which neither man could see from their vantage points. "No fight, Trane. I want Khiry to be happy. Right now, I think she's happy."

Kor nodded slightly at the steering wheel in his hands. He planned to make her happier, if he could get her off this horrid planet, but that wasn't something a man told other men in casual conversation.

"What about Electra?" Trane asked then. "You think it's going to make her happy to pag some alien who loves another woman?"

"Ah, your dog *is* in this fight," Kor mocked. "Got eyes for the exotic lady, have you?"

"Electra knows what she's doing," Jay said. "She's experienced when it comes to breaking hearts. You can get in line, Bay."

"Nice," Trane muttered.

None of them could think of another masculine comment to make, so the discussion ended. They imagined their comrades' thoughts went to finding power coils aboard the ship and confronting Gibson upon their return to Touch Down City when, in fact, each turned their thoughts to women and bedroom things that they'd never admit out loud.

Chapter Twenty-Two

A storm rose over the mountains as the gentlemen guided the three buggies over the drawbridge, but it was far enough away to pose no threat. T-Rex flew into the city and perched atop a church, leaning against the steeple to rub her back while the people below pulled the drawbridge back into place.

Khiry came out of June's bed-and-breakfast house to greet the men who beamed like soldiers returned victorious from war. Gibson wasn't far behind her, but looked disheveled and well-used by the ladies of the town. What Kor found odd was the relatively small number of ladies in the town. They'd only seen June, Ferra, and Bev alive and well so far. June seemed a bit old and matronly—as well as married—for Gibson's tastes. Gibson seemed a bit slimy and useless for Ferra's tastes. That left Bev to do all the work rumpling up the greasy sot.

When Trane saw Gibson approaching the buggies with brow furrowed in concern, he looked to Khiry. "You're back in charge now. Can I do the honors this time?"

"The honors?"

"What the devil is this!?" Gibson roared. He strode from the first buggy toward Kor as if he'd lay hands on the marksman's neck. Half way there, he met Trane's fist against his jaw, solid and cracking something beneath the skin.

"What is this?" Khiry asked, ignoring the writhing man in the dirt. She had to step around him to peer into the nearest buggy at two new, heavy power coils. "Is this what he hid aboard my ship?"

"*Your* ship?" Kor asked.

She grinned at him. "No one else is going to lay claim to the wreck."

"I might," Red giggled from June's doorway. "I've got a lot of good memories on that ship."

"Hey, look who's got something to say," June announced, reaching out to put her arm around Red's ample form.

Khiry was pleased to see Red saying something that wasn't muttered despair, but she didn't really need a reminder of the woman's former personality.

Kor grimaced. Maybe Red had been Gibson's morning entertainment, he thought. Something had pulled the woman back into herself. He looked down at Khiry next to him and breathed in the fresh scent of flowers in her hair. Whatever shampoo June had given her was still lovely.

"This is what he hid on the ship," Kor told her. "There are four more in the other buggies. We tossed out the half used ones from the Instigator. Think these'll get communications up?"

"And then some. Let's get them to the building under the tower before the storm grounds these buggies."

"Fine idea. Trane! Jay! A little further to drive."

* * * * *

It took until after dark to get connections made, cords rewired, cables restrung, and the console cleared of furry rodents that looked remarkably like mice from Earth. The little critters had short teeth, though, and didn't appear to have done any damage beyond building nests of hair and dried grass everywhere. They stared with dark beady eyes as Khiry and Jay worked at wires and computer parts as if they considered the people squatters on their land.

"They tend to chatter a lot," Jay said.

"We've destroyed all their nests."

"No, you've *moved* all their nests. Moved them as if there was room to move in this little building. Didn't you tell Kor he was too kind for his own good just a day ago?"

She grimaced at the thought. That had been a terrifying few minutes. Jay had a good point about the small room they were in right now, though. It might be best to encourage the mice-like vermin to move on. The room couldn't have been seven meters across. Maybe it was a little deeper than that, but not much. They'd be hard pressed to fit everyone in tonight, and that was the plan. Fixing communications had taken too long. Night would be upon them before they got it done, but they wouldn't risk letting a touched or an inhabitant sneak into the city and tear up the place again. So this was the fort they'd defend tonight, with the dragons' help. This was the room twelve people would have to fit in—and share with the rodents.

She smiled at a light-brown, furry creature staring up at her from the console. It sat back on its tiny haunches, holding its pink paws in front of its mouth, ready to run in either direction should she reach for it. In a moment of pity, she offered it a piece of the muffin June had given her for dinner. The little creature stared. So she set the piece of muffin on the console just a few centimeters in front it.

As if it knew exactly how good muffins from humans were, the creature snatched up the morsel, stuffed it in its mouth, and ran like mad down the table leg and across the floor. Jay, lying under the console quite near to the table leg, let out a surprised sound. He'd never admit it was a scream, of course, but she figured it was as close as an alien male came to such a thing.

By the time dusk approached, the few members of the colony and crew joined them in the short building. Khiry heard—and felt—the dragons approach and settle themselves outside. Bev, Mr. and Mrs. Mill, and Ferra sat out of the way. Trane settled Shayla and Red near them. Gibson and Kor paced the small space. Electra stood elegantly beyond anyone's reach, watching Khiry with admiration.

Few leaders were willing to crawl in dust to repair computers for their peoples' safety. She'd never seen her brother or any of his aides do anything so mundane or dirty. Lamahl kept his hands clean and bacteria-free. Ever since the influenza uprisings began in the early years of the century, their mother had protected him from touching anything unclean. Just about everything was considered unclean.

With this thought in her mind, Electra walked the few paces to the console where Khiry now sat on a three-legged stool, and asked, "What can I do to help? I don't want to be in the way, but I want to do what I can to help you."

Khiry smiled over her right shoulder at her. "We've just about got it."

"This is Khiry's strong suit," Jay said. "She's not so good at landing."

Over her left shoulder, Khiry shot him a sour look that suggested he not tease so much. "Is that a mouse by your foot?" she asked.

He merely grinned back. Apparently, the prospect of getting help had put them in a good mood. Electra nodded and walked back to the small space she'd picked out for waiting. She watched how the others waited, watched their anxious faces. Each seemed to predict something different. She wasn't sure what she expected.

Khiry pumped up the power switch on the console and placed its cover down. Then she leaned toward the microphone and said, "Here we go." She flipped a toggle switch labeled "Eldora Moon" and spoke into the mic.

"Eldora Moon, this is Eldora Prime. Are you there?"

A crackle and hiss of space static answered.

She flipped the toggle switch off and back on again. "Eldora Moon, this is Eldora Prime. Are you there?"

"God, save us!" a disembodied voice called back. Its tinny reverberation ricocheted inside all their skulls. "This is Eldora Moon. Is this really Eldora Prime?" His titillation was unmistakable.

"Praise God," Bev said, grabbing the hands of her neighbor June. In her fever, she failed to notice how heavy June's hands were.

"This is Eldora Prime," Khiry said and her smile filled her voice. "It's good to hear you. What station have I reached?"

"This is Authority Station Seven. My commander will want to hear this."

"Wait! Don't leave us! We have an emergency. It's imperative that you let your commander know what danger we're in here. We have no power to get off planet and are under attack nightly by inhabitants of this world. Our numbers are—"

"Wait, wait, I can't type that fast. Let me get this. What regulation is this under?"

"Regulation?" Jay asked.

Khiry waved him away from the console. "I believe an emergency attack is a regulation fifteen hundred."

"But the fifteen hundreds apply to space emergencies," the tinny voice argued.

"Can you do something to clean up the reception?" Gibson asked, rubbing his ears.

Almost all eyes turned on him as if he were crazy. All eyes except June's and Khiry's. June sat in silence, concentrating on her breathing, trying to stay focused for what Gibson had asked of her. She needed to hold on just a few moments longer. Khiry closed her eyes and regulated her breathing, trying every calming technique she could think of so as not to scream at the underling on the other end of the communications cyberlink.

"Sir," she said kindly. "I'm not sure which regulation a terraforming attack falls under because I typically work in space. The leaders of the terraforming colony on Eldora Prime are all dead. Do you understand what kind of emergency we have now?"

There was a pause.

"Tell me you still have the link," Kor whispered.

"Here it is!" the voice shouted over the cyberwaves. "A land emergency attack is in the twenty-one hundreds. I knew I'd studied…wait. Did you say it was a *terraforming* land attack?"

"I want this lad's name and serial number," Trane muttered. "I'm firing him out an airlock the minute I set eyes on him."

"What was that?" the voice asked. A hint of fear had crept into it. This was highly irregular, and he was figuring that out.

"Sir," Khiry said sweetly. "We're in so much danger that the few of us left alive are stressed beyond clear thinking. If you need to get your commander to speak with us, we can wait a minute, maybe two. But we must impress upon you how important it is that you send a transport vessel to save us at first light on the eastern hemisphere of Eldora Prime. Does that make sense to you? First light on the eastern hemisphere."

"I—I don't know what to type that under," he said. "I really must get my commander."

"Thank you so much," Khiry said. "You are our savior, sir. If you can convince your commander to rescue us at first light on the eastern hemisphere, you may be able to save those of us who are left here."

"First light on the eastern hemisphere," he finally repeated.

She sighed in relief.

"I'll be right back," he said. They could hear the sound of his boots tapping out a fading rhythm on a sterile floor somewhere on Eldora Moon Authority Station Seven.

"How can you be so calm?" Gibson hissed at her. His move toward her met with Kor's fist against his chest.

"We will get further with kindness," she said. "That lad is manning a communications station that sits silent a majority of the time. The last thing he expected on his watch was to hear from the missing colonists of Eldora Prime. I couldn't very well bark orders at him and expect him to remember or understand a word of it when he got to his next in command."

"She's right," Electra said as if in defeat. "I'm embarrassed by the bureaucracy we've just heard. Some lad afraid to type up a distress call because he didn't know the codes to use? It's preposterous."

Behind them, the door to the building clicked closed. June had left.

"Stupid woman," her husband said.

"Go get her," Kor ordered.

"Not on your life. She's stupid enough to go out there with inhabitants hunting us, then she gets what she deserves."

Kor sighed and turned for the door. It appeared he'd go get her himself.

"I'll go," Gibson said.

Nothing could have surprised the group more.

"You?" Trane laughed.

"Yes, I *am* the security chief of this little operation."

Kor gave Trane a look that suggested he accompany the "security chief."

"I'll come along, *chief*. Just in case you run into something you can't handle."

Gibson frowned, but didn't offer resistance. He figured Trane would be easy enough to deal with if the dragons stayed calm and out of the picture. The two exited the building and were engulfed in darkness. The door clicked closed behind them.

Shayla reached out to touch Electra's arm, garnering her attention. "Will the USPS save the dragons, too?"

"I don't know. The dragons belong on Eldora Moon, so I imagine they can be convinced to return them there."

Shayla smiled. "I like that. Since you're the USPS's sister, you can make sure they do that, right?"

Electra gave a light laugh. "Well, the United Society for Peace and Strength is bigger than one man. My brother's just the leader on Earth."

"But that gives you power," Shayla said. "Because you have power, you can use it to save people. You can use your position of power to get people home."

Shayla had oversimplified the situation the way a child would, but her point was valid. Jay winked at Electra. He seemed to say, "Just say 'yes'." She blushed, remembering how difficult it was to say "no" to him.

"Eldora Prime," a man's voice barked. "This is Eldora Moon Authority Station Seven, Commander Elden Sharp presiding. To whom am I speaking?"

"This is Eldora Prime," Khiry said, not ready to reveal her identity yet. "We're in danger, Commander. We're under attack—"

"I asked, to whom am I speaking?"

She hesitated. She would say "Rewk" if she knew the leader's last name.

Electra stepped up behind Khiry and put a hand on her shoulder. "I am Electra Endh, sister of Presidente Lamahl Endh. You can verify this with voice recognition software, but I order you not to waste time with such trivialities. My life is in danger the longer you leave me stranded on this planet."

"Miss Endh!" the commander stuttered. "I had no idea. Please forgive—"

"I require transport vessels for twelve people and four dragons of Eldora Moon. These vessels need to land well to the south of Touch Down City in the eastern hemisphere after daybreak."

No response followed her transmission.

"Eldora Moon?"

Again, only space dust answered.

"Commander Sharp, are you there?"

Khiry strained to hear something, even the crackle of static, but nothing filtered through the speaker. She flipped the toggle switch off and on. "Eldora Moon," she said. "This is Eldora Prime. Are you there?"

The console went dead.

The lights followed suit.

The door flew open inwardly, which wasn't supposed to happen, and Red screamed.

Chapter Twenty-Three

For just a second, no one realized anything was wrong with June. In the light cast by the backup generator, yes, she looked bedraggled, but, all things considered, who wouldn't? When it registered for Kor that she was the one who had flung the door open in opposition to its hinges, he raised his gun and pointed it toward her bulging eyes. Her husband had already backed away.

June grabbed Red by her one good hand and pulled her out into the night. Kor's plasma stream blast hit the doorframe a split second too late. Red's stump of an arm waved frantically into the dark as she tried to seek a purchase on the frame, on the building, on Shayla reaching out for her. But that hand was gone and the handicap had no doubt just cost the plump woman her life.

"Trane!" Kor shouted, moving toward the doorway. He stood to the side, his back against the wall. He glanced at the faces staring at him in the room. "Everyone stay in the light," he said. With his gun leading, he turned out into the dark.

Khiry looked up at Jay.

A second passed while she let her brain process it all. She pulled her flashlight from her belt. "All right, then," she said, rising from her stool. "Everyone, over here next to the console." She glanced up at the ceiling to be sure there were no panels or vents to worry about. Its smooth metal surface looked uninterrupted to her.

She saw Junior peering in the doorway and motioned for him to come in. The dragon made movement in the room pretty difficult now, but she liked that idea. Nothing else was getting in.

"Everybody has a flashlight?"

Heads nodded.

"And guns?"

Fewer heads nodded.

"Find a partner who has a gun. Hold hands until I get back."

"Until you get back?" Jay said. "No. You're relieved of duty again. Stay here with—"

"Leaders don't get to step down when things get rough," she said. "Keep Electra safe. She's your ticket to freedom."

He stammered something that would have been a response if she'd stayed long enough to hear it. Instead, she ran out into the night with her flashlight poised to blind anything threatening her and her gun ready to spang it.

The light of the Eldora moon cast a glow over the pavement outside. Onyx waited for her. T-Rex had already taken to the sky, circling, waiting for something they could strike.

"Where's Kor?" she asked Onyx. Of course the dragon only stared down at her. His gray-blue eyes were a deeper blue than normal; he had no trouble seeing in the dark. He reared his head back, ready to blast fire at whatever she pointed to.

Something had bitten June. She needed to find that something and spang it. Or have Onyx cook it. When Onyx growled, she spun to see a large, lumbering black shadow moving toward them. It was immense. It was the lesser black dragon who had carried Rewk to the city two nights before. It was changed into something monstrous. She didn't get to contemplate its hideous features, though. Something behind her shrieked and she spun again. This time she came face to face with Trane. Or what was left of Trane. He leaned his head back and his new gaping maw unhinged itself.

She screamed as she blasted him with the gun in her hand. Khiry shook with the knowledge that she'd spanged a friend. What else was there to do? There certainly wasn't time to mourn. A powerful dragon moved toward her with the same crazed hunger that Trane had. She turned back to face the danger, raising her gun again. *Father in Heaven, save me,* she thought. *Let this gun be powerful enough to damage this thing.* She dreaded the thought of what would become of the people who depended on her if this massive creature got past her and to the little building of easy meals…Well, maybe Jay wouldn't go down so easily. He'd give a good fight.

She'd never seen dragons before her ill-fated trip to Eldora Prime, thus she'd never seen a dragon fight. The minor scuffle in the cargo hold when Onyx had disciplined T-Rex for biting Red had been nothing. Merely a chastisement of sorts. What she witnessed here before the communications tower bordered on cataclysmic.

T-Rex swooped in out of nowhere, pummeling the lesser black with a force that sent the touched creature sprawling. Wings tangled with tails over snapping snouts over scales flashing in the light of the moon. The ground shook with the force of their impact. Onyx let out a roar and beat his front claws against his chest like some angry horror film gorilla. He was certainly big enough to fit the role. But instead of grabbing her up and running away, he charged into the fight.

"No!" Khiry called after him. Like a human male, Onyx ignored her. He was determined to deal with this. One of his own had been changed.

She cocked her weapon, raised it, and waited for an opening. She kept the rolling, fighting, snapping dragons in her sights, waiting for the right one to land in the clear. It just wasn't happening. She dared not fire and miss. When the lesser black snapped hard and clenched its jagged teeth down on T-Rex, a set of howls went up. Khiry couldn't differentiate her own from the chorus. Onyx swatted the lesser black relentlessly with his tail.

T-Rex took a second to shake the shock from her head, and then furrowed her dragon brow and bent her head into the task once more. There was no telling how many minutes were left to her, but she intended to use those minutes killing the creature who'd just damned her. She turned her head and rammed her anterior horns into the lesser black's belly. It let out a wail that sent Khiry to her knees. Onyx backed from the scene, waddling on his massive hind legs in his own dragon disbelief. T-Rex had hit so hard, she'd bent her head in such a way that her regal reddish-black neck had snapped. Her last few minutes had been blessedly free of the horror of the touched.

Onyx reared back his head and spewed forth a cloud of orange flame that engulfed the two bodies. The lesser black screamed in his death throes as his scales and flesh caught fire. The stink of it carried to Khiry in a heartbeat. She covered her nose and nearly screamed herself when Kor ran up behind her and grabbed her around the waist.

"Quickly," he hissed, pulling her toward the communications tower.

She ran with him, smoke stinging her eyes until tears brimmed over to wash the smoke away.

He opened a hatch to let her into the metal shed beneath the tower. It was barely big enough for three or four people and the wiring panels she had repaired there earlier that day. Now only Kor and she stood in the space, panting for breath and leaning against the door as if that could keep out one of the touched if they'd been seen entering this place.

She sobbed, turning toward him. Her flashlight dropped to the dirt floor, rolling just a pace or two away, shining its crisp bluish light on them like a certain and steady spotlight. She cried against his arm. Something familiar, something strong, something warm. He pulled her close, wrapping both arms around her then to offer comfort. The little room was safe so he dropped the gun to the floor. Both of his hands held her against him, letting her weep for lost friends when they were so close to rescue.

"I had to kill Trane," she cried into his chest.

He could barely hear her muffled words, but he understood them.

"An inhabitant killed Trane," he said. "You killed the shell that some demon lived in."

She sobbed some more. "Red's gone. T-Rex is gone. That woman June is gone. How many of us will be here when USPS gets here in the morning?"

He moved then to put his hands to either side of her head. He held her just a small space from him and looked into her lovely brown eyes dripping with tears. "We've already lost people. We'll likely lose a few more by morning. This is how it's going to be. But *you* are strong. I am strong. We're going to make it. I'm going to make sure you make it. Do you understand me, Khiry Okerson? I'm going to ensure you make it off this planet. When help arrives, I'm getting you on one of their ships and getting you to safety."

He pulled her face in close to his and pressed his lips to hers. His kiss was welcome and powerful. Something strong within him seemed to transfer to her in the heat of him. She returned his kiss with vigor, as if she would transfer something strong within her to him. They were good for each other. They matched each other. Their hold tightened. Their kiss deepened like something the touched sought with crazed hunger. She managed to break contact for a second, gazing at his mouth and then into his deep brown eyes.

"What have I been missing?" Khiry asked.

He didn't smile, didn't answer with words, but resumed kissing her, running a hand into her hair to hold her somehow closer.

* * * * *

At some point, he had released her. She had stopped crying for the lives she couldn't retrieve. They stood with their backs against the door staring at the flashlight on the dirt floor, contemplating what to do next.

"I can't stay here until morning," she practically whispered. "I have to check on the others. Jay can't hold off the inhabitants alone."

"The drawbridge is up."

"True." She thought about this and all its implications for a moment. If the drawbridge had remained up, then no new touched or inhabitants would have gotten into the city that day—theoretically. That meant only the creatures who had avoided the civic center cleansing the night before were still a threat. There couldn't be very many left in the city walls. As long as no one lowered the drawbridge. It made her think of Gibson and his treacherous ways. She asked, "What was Gibson doing earlier? When he went out after June? He couldn't have been trying to help her."

"I don't believe he was. I think he arranged what happened to her. There were inhabitants around him, but they weren't attacking him. I think he…fed…June and then Trane to them. He disconnected the power coils and put them back in the buggies. That's why the console stopped working. That's why the lights went out. I'm sure he didn't count on the backup generator charging during the day. We were probably all supposed to die while he waited for morning and the transport vessels to arrive. He'd drive the buggies out to the arriving ships and even have help loading them."

She nodded. "That makes sense. Sounds like his kind of plan." She leaned her head back against the door and looked up at the ceiling of the tiny shed. "And there's really not that much longer until morning."

"Thank God," he said.

She looked over at him. "I think they would have attacked by now if they knew we were here."

"That's not what I mean," he said.

She frowned. "I don't understand."

"I'm thankful for morning because this nearness to you…this closeness…after kissing you like that…"

She blushed. "We were emotionally distressed."

"No, we were finally together." He paused a beat. "And we'll be together again."

Gulping back a sort of panic at the thought that raced through her mind, she said, quietly. "We're together right now."

He looked at her seriously. "Don't tempt me, Khiry. You have no idea how badly I want…how much I wish we could…it's just so dangerous out there. Anything could tear through this door at any moment."

She nodded, and then frowned. "I hear something."

"So do I," he worried.

They pressed their ears to the door, slowing their breathing to hear the whir of something large and overhead.

"Power in the communications tower?" she whispered.

"I don't think so," he whispered back.

Then her eyes opened wide in alarm. "Oh no, it's engines."

"Ion engines," he clarified.

"USPS already sent ships."

"They're landing ships at night," he murmured in incredulity.

"Oh, Kor, they sound way too close."

Chapter Twenty-Four

The ships landing outside the city drew more than the people from the communications tower and building. While they, of course, peered out hesitantly, checking for things that go bump in the night, calling in hushed tones to one another as they rendezvoused near a recently abandoned warehouse, the inhabitants and a few touched ran for the landing sites, forgetting to stick to the roadway.

"Praise your god," Jay said, "but you're a sight for sore eyes. Good to see you alive and well."

Khiry colored under the alien's obvious sentiment, but no one could see that in the darkness. Even with their glow of LED beams pointed this way and that, spilling pools of light first on the stone of the building, then the asphalt beneath their feet, then the clothing of a comrade, then a dragon's shimmering obsidian scales, no one could see any one feature for any length of time.

"Someone needs to get to the drawbridge and climb up to wave the ships off," Kor said. "They can't land in the mine fields."

"Is that what we're hearing?" Bev the colonist asked. "Ships? Jay here said it was ships."

"Jay's right," Electra said with controlled frustration. Apparently, she was tired of giving Bev information. She looked to Khiry. "Do you think we can get communications working again?"

Khiry was shaking her head. "Gibson disconnected the power coils."

"Then we reconnect them," Jay said.

"He wasn't too particular about the cables," Kor said. "Cut through them with I don't know what. Tagger should've been electrocuted twice over."

"Then we repair the cables, too," Jay said. "We've got to get a message to those ships. They're going to blow up and there goes our chance at escape off this blasted rock."

"Relax," Electra said. "Surely the captains will notice the first ship that explodes and realize what's happening."

"Yes, but will they figure out what regulation that goes under in time to back off?" Bev asked.

Electra narrowed her eyes to glare at the woman. "They won't endanger their crews to land in a minefield. That's common sense."

"And the one or two that land successfully?" Khiry asked. "What happens to the landing parties that set foot on Eldora Prime? Whoever doesn't blow up tonight will be touched or food for an inhabitant by morning. These people are flying into hell just like we did, only they're doing it at the worst possible time in the worst possible site. We've got to find a way to warn them. Kor's plan is valid for the moment. Shayla, can you get Junior to the drawbridge? Kor, will you go with her? Protect them and help them?"

He nodded. "Of course. Shayla?"

The diminutive lady with the dragon at her side smiled then. "Of course. It will be my honor to serve to protect." She sounded like Electra. Had she been taking lessons the past few days? It occurred to Khiry that Electra would make an excellent representative to meet the ships coming in, but, for the moment, the regal sister of Presidente Lamahl Endh didn't seem to be volunteering for the job. "Let's waste no time," Shayla said.

Kor tossed a glance full of meaning and warning to Khiry as he and Shayla turned to go. The doctor Ferra jogged a few steps to catch up to them and the dragon that lumbered after them. "I'll come with you. I'm sure you'll need a doctor at some point."

Khiry and Jay didn't watch them go, but turned to their task at the communications building. Khiry looked to Mr. Mill. "Can you help us get the power coils back out of the buggy and into position by the shed?"

"My pleasure." He seemed entirely too happy for a man who'd been living under the strain of constant fear for years. Khiry wondered if the loss of his wife truly freed him so much. "Until you folks came along, I had no hope of getting off Eldora Prime. When you got that console working in the night, hope came back to live right in here." He pounded on his chest as if to indicate his heart. "I believe you can do it again."

Khiry offered him the most reassuring smile she had at the moment. It would be more difficult to conjure once they saw the mess Gibson had made of the power coil cables.

"Pegger!" Jay muttered with feeling. "Did the brownspotter melon have to do so much damage getting them out? I mean, really, was that necessary? Was he trying to damn us?"

"Yes," Khiry answered. "Kor and I think his plan was to leave us here to die while he got out with his power coils. These things are worth a fortune to the right warring tribe."

Jay rubbed his hands over his face. "All right, I need those flashlights and lanterns. Just keep the evil beasties away and I'll get this solved." He flashed Khiry a confident grin as Electra moved first to point a flashlight down on the mess of cables and cords. "You guys don't call me Mozart for nothing. Let me do something creative."

Khiry snorted. The moniker referred more to his insanity than his creativity, but she elected not to say so in front of those unfamiliar with his bizarre ways. *Let them be inspired or encouraged or whatever by this,* she thought. She stood

back a few paces and watched him play with wires
enlivened by the backup generator.

*   *   *   *   *

Jay failed.

It really was as simple as that. By the time the first ship
touched down and triggered a host of landmines beneath
the dirt and grass surface, rocking the ground clear back to
the communications building where they stood in despair,
Jay hadn't even made a dent in the maze of wires that
sparked and bit at him from time to time.

To be fair, the failure wasn't entirely his fault. He'd
been distracted greatly when Mr. Mill died. The unit of
five, dragon and all, had turned their attention from the
pool of LED haze where Jay worked to the buggy where
the man shouted his last curse word. Bev turned in time to
see the power coil that the man cursed fall in its crushing
staccato bounce. First it hit the sprawling Mr. Mill's head,
then his chest, then the ground next to him, before tottering
into a roll toward the group. Onyx had reacted by then and
clamped a front claw down on the device to stop it in its
tracks. It was too late for Mr. Mill. It had been too late the
second he lost his footing and his grip.

Electra had blanched at the sight of the man's crushed
face. Jay and Khiry wasted precious minutes carrying the
body to the other side of the communications tower. It
wasn't very far away, but it made them feel as though their
latest offering to the inhabitants was at least a few meters
further from their vulnerable group.

Thus, when the sounds of the first explosions reached
them, Jay didn't have the power coils reinstalled yet. Khiry
couldn't communicate with the ships in the air. They

realized with chagrin that Kor and Shayla must have failed at communication as well.

Khiry muttered something about the United Society for Peace and Strength under her breath.

"You *did* tell them not to land near the city," Jay said. "You can't feel responsible for this."

"Yes, but as someone once told me, responsibility doesn't matter once people start dying. The people aboard that ship are still dead, whether I take responsibility for their deaths or someone in the USPS does. And you can bet no one in the USPS's going to take responsibility for it."

Khiry's last statement rang in Electra's mind while the group formed their next plan. It distracted her so that she didn't hear the things Bev, Khiry, and Jay said to each other. Khiry was right, of course. No one in the United Society for Peace and Strength would take the blame for losing a ship with however many dozens of lives on board while landing on a hostile planet. They would seek another scapegoat, as Captain Marlon had once suggested making Khiry.

The captain had understood the United Society for Peace and Strength's mindset. So had Gibson. Nothing happens without someone to blame it on. Nothing happens without someone to punish for it. She looked across the group of busy planning voices to Khiry, the strong leader. Khiry would be imprisoned if they got off this planet.

Electra wondered what she could do to prevent that.

"Are we going then?" Bev asked, almost impatiently.

Khiry nodded. "If Kor hasn't come back with different news. At first light. We take this buggy with its coils. We get to the drawbridge and offer them to whatever ship and officers are still alive. And we get off this planet. If Kor comes back saying they all died out there before sunrise, well, then we get these coils and the others onto the colony ship and we get off this paggin' planet."

"Six coils won't be enough to fuel the reactions for their engines," Jay said, as if repeating a tired argument.

"It will be enough to get out of atmo and fire us toward Eldora Moon," Khiry explained. "The rest is just coasting. It'll take three or four days, unless they see us and pull us in with a tractor beam."

Electra nodded at that. Of course the United Society for Peace and Strength would see them. Of course they'd pull them in. Especially if all the ships reaching Eldora Prime this early morning failed to report back.

Her blood felt cold inside her body at the thought. She realized that she didn't really fear for the United Society for Peace and Strength officers on board the ships. She feared for her new comrades who would be collected by the tractor beam and brought before whatever commander of whatever station they ended up near on Eldora Moon. She imagined the bureaucratic conversation in her mind, seeing Khiry and Kor in separate rooms and at cold metal tables with their hands bound by metal bars behind their backs.

"Tell me again why you failed to warn our ships of the danger on Eldora Prime," the commander would ask.

"I did warn them," Khiry would say. "Over the communications system."

"We have a recording of that."

The commander would play a cold, tinny recording with all the appropriate bits deleted to protect his career and win him a reward from Presidente Lamahl Endh.

"You're missing information in that recording," Khiry would say. "Our link had been damaged and recently repaired."

"So you admit that you were unable to warn our ships of the danger on Eldora Prime?"

In Kor's sterile room, the commander would put the question to him. Why had he failed to warn the United Society for Peace and Strength of Eldora Prime's inherent danger? Kor, being saucier than Khiry, would say something to the effect of, "We tried," or "We didn't think you'd be too stupid to figure out that a colony that's been out of communication for a dozen or so years suddenly calling for help might have an inherent danger."

Electra would eventually be presented to her brother, her own testimony ascribed to stress, over-active imagination, torture by the resistance jumpers who'd smuggled her aboard the Instigator, and the need for medication. A doctor would talk about Stockholm Syndrome and prescribe some psychotropic drug. They'd put her in a comfortable, pretty home in Nevada where she could watch the wildfire that burned constantly along the length of California and she'd soon forget Khiry, Kor, and the talented alien Jay.

Snapping out of the horrible daydream, she stared at the group lugging the power coil back into the buggy before her. The power of disillusionment descended on her like a suffocating cloak. She realized she had served the wrong master.

Chapter Twenty-Five

Kor had no such epiphany. He already knew that the United Society for Peace and Strength would likely try to imprison them, but he had no intention of getting to that point. His family had served the United Society for Peace and Strength as public, professional, and proficient assassins and bodyguards for three generations. He had only recently broken tradition and "gone tagger" as some said. He figured he still served the government because he didn't join the resistance. He didn't openly support the resistance or even give their members easy berth. Considering the United Society for Peace and Strength's suicidal attempt at retrieving Electra Endh from Eldora Prime and certain hostiles, he had no doubt he was being labeled a traitor. A disappointment to his family.

Trying to warn ships against landing in a minefield wouldn't make up for his perceived crime getting to this planet and surviving on it. If he survived.

He pulled Shayla and Ferra into the depths of the city. He led them toward the others where they could form a new plan. Morning was nigh and at least one vessel had managed to land mostly on the road. Lowering its ramp had allowed a swarm of inhabitants to grab uniformed officers before the creatures realized the light spilling out of the ship was as bright as day and stabbed their multiple eyes like daggers. He still heard the shrieking and wailing. He still saw the inhabitants carry their prey off to the mountains in the chaos of approaching dawn. Dawn that had at some point in his life seemed pretty and gray-blue like a dragon's eyes.

That was another lifetime ago. On another planet.

"Kor," Jay hissed from the dimness. He stood on guard a few meters from the communications building. Kor approached and grasped hands with the alien. Shayla,

Ferra, and Junior watched in solemn silence, a testimony to what they'd seen in the dark morning hours.

"Where's Onyx?" Kor asked.

The creature unfolded from camouflage not three paces from them, his wings unwrapping from their clever hold on a building's marble walls.

"We lost Mr. Mill to an accident," Jay said. "But Bev, Electra, and Khiry are resting in the building." He jerked his head in the direction of the communications shed with its gaping doorway. LED and lantern light spilled from the damaged maw.

Kor nodded. "Have you thought of what we do next?"

"We've agreed on something."

Kor was visibly relieved. "Let's hear it."

"It hinges on there being a ship that made it down. Any crew or vessel that can lift off again."

"There's one. Landed on the road. Not all of her crew was taken."

Jay nodded at that and began explaining the idea of taking all the power coils as a sort of peace offering to the United Society for Peace and Strength crew. Show them the coils and Electra. Let them rescue the small party and the presidente's sister, and take the coils as payment for a job well done. Kor particularly liked the part about paying off the officers. It just might save their skins.

"It's a sound plan," Kor agreed. "Round up the buggies. Are all the coils in them?"

"Just these two that Gibson started stealing last night."

"Then we've got four more to load."

* * * * *

Jay pretended not to notice Kor and Khiry's reunion. Onyx watched the two embrace with confusion.

"Don't think there's time for that this morning," Bev said crassly. "Aren't we going out to meet the USPS?"

Ferra had helped her from her place sleeping on the dust floor and answered. "Only one ship made a safe landing. We'll be approaching that one. You could help load a power coil—"

"Oh, no. Not after what happened to Junie's man. I'm not getting anywhere near those things. They're too dangerous."

"Bev," Ferra said, wanting to calm her, but not understanding the problem.

"That's the accident I mentioned," Jay explained. "Power coil fell on Mr. Mill while he tried to move it."

"And no one bothered to bury him," Bev snapped. "Just carted his body off into the dark for some beast to come feed on. Like he's dog food."

Dog food, Khiry thought. That was something odd for this colony to be missing. Dogs. She had been too preoccupied with survival to notice anything missing before, but, if one stopped to think about it, where were the peoples' pets? Surely a terraforming colony was allowed pets. And children. Did the inhabitants take those early on because they were weak?

"We have no time to bury the number of dead we're amassing," Kor said simply. He had less patience for Bev's worries than Electra did. "When you die, we'll leave you for the beasts as well."

Bev gasped.

"If you don't want that, you best keep up and contribute," he said. "Now let's load the power coils. Get moving."

She huffed out the doorway he gestured toward, tossing a contentious "I have to relieve myself" over her shoulder as she stomped.

"Groups," Kor suggested, signaling to Khiry.

The small collective of women gathered to the side of the communications building to deal with nature. Electra marveled at how base her existence had become, yet how functional. She almost laughed at the fact that Khiry, their leader, could pull down her pants while holding a plasma gun. And then could pull them back up again.

"Are we ready?" Khiry finally asked.

Bev stood a few paces from the building with her hands on her hips. Her green jumpsuit hugged her frame when the breeze pushed it and her short brown hair flew just wildly enough to get in her mouth as she spoke. "I don't think I should be used by a bunch of jumpers to do manual labor."

Apparently, having failed to get her way in front of Kor, she would try it in front of Khiry. Like a petulant child playing off each parent to see which would let her have a cookie before dinner.

Shayla frowned. "But jumpers are from the resistance. We're not in the resistance."

There's the child, Khiry thought. *And the childlike innocence that should shut this woman up.*

"Would you prefer manual labor or inhabitant bait?" Khiry asked.

Electra had been trying to form some sort of response, some sort of speech that a good leader like her brother would expect from her. Words escaped her this morning, and she appreciated Khiry's. She smiled in amusement.

"Ladies," Jay called. "I'm going to the back of the compound."

"Compound?" Khiry asked.

She met him at the back where the buggy waited with its precious load of power. "All aboard," he said. "Let's drive this over to the main power grid."

"Where's Kor?"

"Went ahead to flush any 'unmentionables' out of the shadows."

Ferra shuddered.

Chapter Twenty-Six

Kor performed his duty well, attracting an inhabitant from the shadows of a doorway not four blocks from their starting point. He let out a shout that they heard before the buggy was clear of the communications building. As they rounded its corner, Khiry saw him on the street ahead. She shivered at the sight of a humanoid body raised on eight tall, muscular, sloped legs that moved with jerking, unpredictable motions. The thing tried to stay in the shadows, shrieking and using one front leg to shield its hideous face when it yanked itself into the blocks of sunlight afforded by breaks in the ravaged buildings.

"Catch up to him!" Khiry shouted to Jay.

"No!" Bev screamed. "Are you mad? That thing will turn on us when it finishes him!"

Electra shushed the woman, but Khiry had already acted. She backhanded Bev across the face with her plasma streamer gun. Bev's initial squeal gave way to the sound of sudden silence as she fell to the floor of the buggy, between the two upright power coils. If she was lucky, they might fall and crush her.

"Go!" Khiry ordered. Onyx took to the sky, the pavement seeming to groan at the push of his back legs and then sigh at the absence of his massive bulk. The crew in the buggy involuntarily ducked at the heavy beat of his wings once, twice, thrice as he lifted up into the air, stirring dirt and loose debris into their already unkempt hair. Junior turned his snout to watch his elder climb into the overcast area of the sky.

Khiry couldn't imagine he could get his wingspan between the buildings. She remembered T-Rex slamming into the lesser black dragon the night before, pummeling and rolling it like a rag doll despite its super-dragon weight.

Onyx might try that with this inhabitant, but how? There just wasn't room.

Jay pressed on the buggy's accelerator, building speed slowly as the solar-powered buggy was wont to do. Khiry worried at this as well. She wondered briefly if they'd be able to maintain velocity in the shadowy areas between the buildings. It was a flaw in their whole plan. They certainly couldn't stop there. Jay would have to be precise in his braking.

Ferra leaned down in the buggy to check on Bev, but no one paid attention to that. The others focused on the fight scene in the street ahead. The inhabitant's bulky abdomen and head were only the size of a large man—maybe an overweight large man—but its legs with their tufts of prickly hair extended its size, allowing it to fill the space between teetering lamp posts. The breadth made the thing difficult to fight, gave it the ability to sweep at Kor from impossible angles.

Kor figured out quickly that his flashlight's beam in its eyes was not as effective in the shadows of day as it was in the pitch black of night, so he dropped the tool and used both hands to hoist his plasma streamer canon to shoulder height. With a Herculean shout, he pressed the trigger in one long bolt of streaming power, raking the beast's head and abdomen with the cutting blast.

The inhabitant screamed into its destruction. Black blood and stinking internal fats rained in the street. Kor ducked his head to keep the disgusting gore off his face, out of his mouth and eyes. The creature's legs began dropping with heavy, cracking thuds before him.

"We'll need a new route," Jay grimaced.

"I know a way there," Ferra said, all business despite the nerve-wracking scene they'd just watched. For some reason, seeing one lone human man stand up to an inhabitant—and destroy it utterly—gave her confidence.

Kor jogged toward the buggy, motioning for them to turn down the brightly lit street to their left. Ferra nodded. "He's right. Turn here."

* * * * *

They moved with great efficiency. No one said it, but those who were conscious feared the United Society for Peace and Strength ship's crew might assume all hands lost and lift off without searching the city. Kor's last-minute decision to lower the drawbridge once daylight dawned and the demonic among them headed into the mountains should have ensured at least an investigation, but, who knew how thorough the skeleton crew would be. Khiry glanced to Electra. Hopefully they would be very thorough.

While no one mentioned the other threat, all eyes glanced from time to time toward the sky to the north. Onyx had flown into a dark mass of clouds that moved slowly, but moved slowly toward them. None of them doubted the inhabitants sat in their hiding places among the foothills just waiting for the storm to blot out the sun and provide easy access to this meal on wheels.

Kor caught Khiry glancing to the sky as they loaded the last of six power coils into the buggy. "Authority has no idea what the storm brings. If they're out searching the city, they're easy pickings for the inhabitants."

Khiry climbed aboard a power coil. "Let's go! Everyone on now."

Bev stirred painfully from a corner where they'd propped her up.

Khiry looked back at Kor. "If they're too stupid to learn fast, then we have that fewer to deal with at the ship."

"And the ship will be overrun."

She shook her head as Jay eased the buggy into groaning motion. "We'll cross that bridge when we come to it."

"We'd move faster walking," Jay muttered.

Electra sat next to him and gave him the most encouraging smile she could muster under the circumstances. "I don't know about you, but I don't think I could walk very fast carrying one of these coils."

He flashed her a grin. An exotic woman with power *and* a sense of humor. He'd like to get another night with her in his bed. Considering they returned her to her life with the United Society for Peace and Strength this morning, he doubted he'd get that chance again.

Kor leaned over the coil he sat on to look into the driver's section. "Tell me we can coax this thing to go faster."

"Just getting up speed now."

"This is not speed. We're crawling."

"We're carrying seven people and six power coils. Anything you feel like throwing out?" Jay asked hotly.

Khiry jerked her head toward the back of the vehicle where Bev moaned. "Trane would make that an easy decision."

Kor shook his head. "She might be annoying, but we can't leave her behind for certain death."

"We should have asked Onyx to carry a couple power coils," Electra said.

Khiry smacked her hand to her head. "You're absolutely right. We've been using him as a guard when he has the strength of ten of us.

"What's faster? Stopping to explain what we want of him or driving on?" Jay asked.

"Stopping and sleeping would be faster than this," Kor muttered. "Are you sure this buggy's sound?"

Jay cursed under his breath. "It's just weighed down is all. But I can't imagine you'll get your point across that you want to make a packhorse of him. And what will the USPS crew think of a dragon showing up with Eldora Moon power coils in hand?"

"We'll be with him," Khiry said.

"How do you know they're from Eldora Moon?" Electra asked. "Gibson never said where he'd got them from and these don't have a neat little label on them to say where they're from. They're contraband for a blender army for certain."

"Sounds easiest," Kor supplied. "Gibson's one for the path of least resistance."

"There's that," Jay said. "And I fired them up for the power grid yesterday and for the console last night. Every power coil has a signature hum. These are manufactured on Eldora Moon."

"You can tell that by their hum," Khiry said, not quite believing him.

"Hey, I'm Mozart, Baby. I don't just *work* on this stuff. It speaks to me. It sings to me."

Kor gave Khiry an uncertain look. "Wasn't Mozart deaf?"

"Naw. Some other composer was deaf."

"Beethoven," Shayla supplied.

She was the last person they expected to know such a thing. Kor smiled beneath his beard and, as if to close the conversation, hopped off the slow-moving buggy. "Stay here," he joked.

Jogging with some purpose in his steps, he ran ahead to the fountain near the front of the city. Khiry could see the open drawbridge beyond the massive stone and water structure. Kor set his hand gun on the fountain's lip and pulled his plasma streamer canon from its carrying holster on his back as he stepped over the tall lip and into the water. He set this larger weapon next to the smaller one and submerged quickly. They all watched, feeling varying levels of voyeurism, as he surfaced, shaking his soaking locks and used his hands to scrub down his well-defined arms and chest. He didn't take the time to remove any clothing. He washed everything—t-shirt, khaki pants, boots, and skin—getting soaked all the way through. Khiry couldn't imagine that would be comfortable.

"We're going to get soaked in this storm any minute," Ferra said, as if questioning the man's actions.

The buggy had moved alongside the fountain by the time Kor hopped out and replaced the larger canon weapon in its holster on his back. He grabbed up the smaller gun and reached for the side of the buggy, swinging himself easily back to his place on the power coil. He dripped.

Flashing Khiry an easy smile from beneath the wet tendrils of his beard he explained, "I feel better without that thing's insides caked and stinking all over me."

Electra laughed lightly. It was something one of her officers would have never done or said. She found a sadness settling in her stomach at the thought of leaving this band of taggers. If taggers could adequately describe them.

Chapter Twenty-Seven

The wind reached them before the dark of the storm did. It seemed to give them a sort of push across the drawbridge and toward the hulking ship on the road. Shayla held up her shawl as if it were a sail, as if it would help push them faster. Onyx saw this and understood. His favorite human and her friends wished to get this self-moving box to the flying box on the dirt ahead. And they wished to go faster than the plodding pace they'd been keeping.

He moved behind the buggy and put both front claws to its back bumper. With a grace that no one aboard had anticipated from the waddling creature, he pushed, increasing their speed easily. Shayla clapped her hands to Junior's happy barking sounds. Onyx grumbled something at Junior that obviously reminded the smaller dragon to stay on the dirt path. He looked down to check the placement of his large back feet before continuing his excited emissions.

Of course the ship they moved toward was too large to fit on the simple width of the dirt road that the colonists had used to get to and from the Uranium mines in the mountains. Its hull overhung the road by a good thirty meters in both directions. It was a good eighty meters long lengthwise down the road. It matched the Instigator in size. What had saved this bright and shiny metallic beacon of hope was its landing gear that extended on two strong, thick pillars near the front of the hull, on a single thick pillar that rested on a flat footlike platform in the middle, and on two strong, thick pillars near the back of the hull. These obviously retracted for flight, as if the vessel needed to be aerodynamic in space. For the moment, their height kept the bulk of the ship up off the landmines to either side of the road and safe from explosions.

The ship's ramp lay open at an angle like a giant metal tongue unrolled to tempt unwary victims up into the glow of the underbelly between the front legs and middle pillar. This was the entrance that the group found their eyes fixed on. This was the promise of escape from the planet of horror and death.

Khiry felt her stomach flop over itself. Was that excitement or warning? The United Society for Peace and Strength would not welcome her once they heard her name; heard that she'd piloted the Instigator away from Eldora Moon with weapons trained on an ACI team.

Kor signaled to Onyx to stop the buggy as they approached the edge of the hull. The ship loomed above them now, resplendent in the sunlight.

"Hello!" he shouted.

Khiry jumped down from the buggy, pointing at Ferra. "Will you watch over Shayla for us, please?"

The woman nodded. Junior hovered near the back of the buggy where Shayla and Ferra sat and watched his elder walk with Khiry and Kor toward the ship's ramp. They hadn't gone four or five paces before a voice boomed over some kind of communications device. Shayla threw her hands to her ears and huddled against Ferra. Junior ducked against the buggy.

"State your names and your business."

Khiry shook her head as if rattling her eardrums back in place. Kor reached up to dig a finger in one ear. "I hope they turn that off," he said.

"What?" she asked.

"Great," he muttered. He called up to the ship. "That's too loud! We're with the terraformers. We're safe. Can you send out a representative to talk to us?"

A pause answered him. Then the voice boomed over the communications system again. "This is agreeable."

The group ducked in unison as if avoiding some low-flying raptor. "We're not in space," Electra moaned, rubbing her ears.

Khiry and Kor waited with Onyx at their side while a uniformed man marched down the ramp. He carried a weapon, of course, and a hand-held computer for recording the proceedings. Electra recognized the make and model of the three-year-old device. Was there nothing new on Eldora Moon? As the man approached, the storm's wind whisked his pointy gray cap off his head. It swirled as if of its own volition on some imaginary roller coaster ride into the distance. The man pursed his lips in consternation.

"What is this creature?"

"A dragon of Eldora Moon," Khiry answered. "He's safe."

The officer assessed the dragon with a quick glance, decided to believe the young lady, and holstered his weapon. He tapped out something on the computer device in his hand and then asked. "What are your names?"

"Our names?" Kor asked. "Don't you want to know what attacked your ship? Don't you want Electra Endh? Don't you want to know what happened to the thousands of terraformers you put here twenty years ago? Don't you want—"

The man hadn't looked up from the little screen in his hand yet. He merely interrupted with, "What are your names?"

"Are you a cyborg?" Khiry asked.

This time the man did look up. He met her gaze squarely and with irritation. "I am an officer of the United Society for Peace and Strength, Miss, and I don't appreciate your condescension. Now tell me your names before I decide to leave you here on this obviously hostile planet."

She raised an eyebrow at his suggestion. He'd die before he got back up the ramp.

"I am Khiry Okerson."

He started tapping something on the computer device, but stopped mid-tap. He looked back at her eyes. "Khiry Okerson? Of the Instigator?"

She smiled as pleasantly as possible. "I have assumed command of that ship now that our traitor captain is dead."

Her words didn't matter. They weren't part of the answer he was after. He looked to the muscular man beside her. "And you?"

"I am John Ashley McCormick the third."

The officer frowned at that. "Yes…also of the Instigator. Your service to the USPS has been well noted." Pause. "In the past."

The officer began tapping quickly on the computer pad. They waited as patiently as their frazzled nerves allowed. The scent of musty earth rose up with the swirling of the wind. Something in the distance howled. It was just a matter of time before the storm unleashed its fury and the inhabitants took advantage of its cover.

"We have little time," Khiry finally suggested. "The storm will provide enough darkness for the beasts on this planet—"

"I'll hear no fairy tales, Miss Okerson. You're wanted for treason against the USPS. As are you, Mr. McCormick. You should cooperate—"

As if someone on board the ship had assessed the storm and agreed with Khiry, a disembodied voice boomed from the speakers above: "Get them aboard." The suddenness of the volume startled the crew again, causing them to jump.

Kor raised his eyebrows at the officer. "Not so pleasant, is it?"

"What?"

"We have power coils that a traitor on our ship stole from Eldora Moon," Kor said loudly, changing the subject quickly. "If someone can help us bring them aboard, you'll look like a hero for bringing the contraband home."

The officer frowned. He'd caught bits of Kor's speech as he regained his hearing. "The two of you are traitors. I'll have no trickery from you. I'll investigate on my own—"

"You don't understand," Kor said. "There are more pressing issues than treason and misunderstandings. You're going to die out here when that storm hits."

"Are you threatening me?" he asked, moving his hand to his weapon. "I'll have to record that you resisted arrest. Your family name is already sullied enough. Think of—"

With his eyes on Kor, he didn't see Khiry move like lightning beside him. She palmed her gun and powered it simultaneously. Its power stream shot through his brain cleanly and he hit the ground in less than a second. She bent down to take the weapon from his belt.

"Was that necessary?" Kor asked. "No doubt his comrades are watching."

"They've already invited us aboard."

She turned to the nervous crew behind her. "Jay! We need to get those coils on board the ship."

A blast of wind and sideward rain hit them. Clouds obscured the sun. A wail and shriek went up from the hillside to the east.

"Fast!" she yelled. "Shayla! Get in the ship! In the light!"

Shayla scrambled down from the buggy as rain pelted her from the side. Junior helped. But as she turned to run for the ship, turned in the wrong direction in her confusion and hurry, she bumped into a waiting inhabitant. It grabbed her in its thick, hairy legs and pulled her toward its opening maw. Her scream rent their nerves asunder.

"Shayla! No!" Khiry yelled. Kor grabbed her around the waist, pulling her toward the ramp and the light of the ship. Junior pulled at Shayla but the inhabitant was stronger. Ferra grabbed the young dragon by his arm and tugged him toward the ship. Jay cursed as the alien equivalent to adrenaline powered his muscles to lift a power coil out of the buggy. Electra shoved one over the side and jumped down next to it. She couldn't lift it beyond that.

"No," Jay called to her. "Leave it. Just run. Run for the ship."

Onyx saw what they did. He understood. The heavy black and gray cylinders were to go on the ship. It must be important, his dragon brain reasoned. He grabbed up two of them and lifted them into the ship's hold. He rolled them carelessly across the metal floor, not noticing that they bowled over two members of the United Society for Peace and Strength, crushing them where they fell. He turned back to the buggy, grabbing a coil from Jay and rolling it across the ship's floor. Nobody died this time. But when he turned to get another, Jay was gone. The alien's shout faded in the distance, carried away by an inhabitant already feasting as it ran on six of eight legs. Onyx grabbed a fourth and fifth coil, barking a dragon order at Junior. Ferra had released the younger dragon to drag the unconscious Bev out of the buggy. Luckily, Bev never came to. Ferra was not so fortunate. Both fell victim to swarming inhabitants. Tossing the two coils onto the ship, Onyx turned to Junior and swept him toward the ship with his powerful wings. His long, regal tail swatted an inhabitant away.

The three stood at the lip of the vessel's ramp—Kor, Khiry, and Electra—staring at a uniformed officer with medals and patches depicting honors and awards all up and down his arms. His pointy gray cap sported one dangling medal that spoke of having bagged a number of jumpers. In his hands, he held a plasma streamer canon about one model older than Kor's and trained on Kor's chest. His hand shook. *Funny,* Khiry thought. *I'd probably target the dragons if I were him, not the human with his hands in the air.*

"We don't take jumpers on an Authority vessel," the man sneered through his self-important snarl. He hadn't heard the conversation of the other officer on the ramp below. He didn't know yet that he had Khiry Okerson and John Ashley McCormick of the Instigator standing in front of him. All he knew was someone had blown up the other ships in his armada in the dark of morning, and these survivors from the colony seemed as likely as any to be the culprits. "If you think you can fire on Authority ships and then order us around, you've got another—"

Electra raised her chin like the princess of power she was and met the officer's eyes. "Do you know who I am? Do you recognize me?"

The stunned man stammered a response. Of course he recognized her. He lowered his weapon as if it were a heavy, thick plate in heavy, thick water.

"These people are not jumpers. They're not members of the resistance. They're members of the United Society for Peace and Strength's terraforming task force who have risked life and limb to rescue me from certain death. You would be wise to let them aboard, make them comfortable, offer them every convenience."

The officer continued his stream of mostly unintelligible gibberish in his hurry to acquiesce. Another officer looked to the dragons beyond Kor and Khiry but safely within the bath of light from the ship. "And what of the dragons, Miss Endh?"

"They are to be returned to Eldora Moon," she stated, as if he were an idiot for thinking otherwise.

"Of course. Of course. Bring them aboard."

"How many in your ship's complement?" she asked next.

The officer directly before her stopped stammering and thought about this. Obviously, this required subtraction. "Three, Miss Endh. We had a few casualties in the night."

"Where are your casualties now?"

"In the sick bay."

"And you're certain they're dead?"

He frowned at such a strange question. "Well, yes."

She didn't smile. "The inhabitants of this planet have a propensity for not-quite-killing their victims."

The officer's eyes went wide. "Mangor!" he shouted. "Check sick bay. Check each body."

"Tell him to spang each body," Electra ordered.

The officer cringed, but obeyed.

The ship rocked slightly as Onyx stepped aboard with the younger dragon weeping beside him. The officer moved quickly to press the right code to close the ramp, sealing them safely inside and the inhabitants of the planet out.

Chapter Twenty-Eight

Khiry dropped next to Kor at the back of the bridge and listened to Electra giving orders to the two officers. It was certainly bigger than the Instigator's bridge. It would have been intimidating with its shiny black metallic floor and smooth paneled walls of well-ordered buttons and switches if she'd been a novice.

As it was, she glanced around the ample room with appreciation for its cleanliness. It may have been stark and sterile with a lingering scent of disinfectant, but it wasn't going to trip anyone like the Instigator did on a regular basis. Of course, the scent of disinfectant now mixed with the limestone and earthy scent of dragons that sat calmly out of the way at the front of the bridge. Onyx watched the humans solemnly. From the windows at this section of the bridge, Junior watched the inhabitants swarming the buggy and single power coil they'd left behind on the ground below. The young creature still couldn't use human speech, but the sounds in his throat mimicked a song she'd heard recently. Her mind filled in the words to a melody the wild beast hummed.

Over in Killarney
Many years ago,
Me mither sang a song to me
In tones so sweet and low.

Her heart ached for poor Shayla and she knew she'd crumble under despair if she listened too closely to the weeping dragon, if she thought too deeply on friends she'd been flying with for years. She forced her thoughts to turn to what was in front of her. She forced herself to focus on the shapes in the brightness that contrasted so vividly to the shadow on the Instigator. Even the windows Junior worried about were more impressive than the Instigator's, molding seamlessly into the curved, clean, sparse bulkhead in front of the main console that stretched in one efficient bank of controls and monitors across the front of the bridge. Swiveling seats that looked extremely comfortable lined the console at reasonable spacings, offering smart-looking stations for crew members. Of course, at the moment, crew members were in short supply.

Desperate to keep her mind on the present, she spoke quietly to Kor. "Do you think three men can get a ship of this size out of atmosphere?"

"They've got older model computers, but still better equipment than we had on the Instigator. I think they could do it with just one."

She nodded at the wisdom in what he said. "I can't believe it's over. I can't believe we're safe."

"Ah, I'll believe we're safe when I hear one of these Authority officers release us to find a new ship to serve on. Electra's not at full form over there. Look at her shake."

Khiry watched the lovely woman for Kor's observed weakness. Sure enough, Electra showed signs of post traumatic stress disorder. Khiry muttered a curse under her breath. "If I could speak with her…" She let her voice trail. Somehow, she knew Kor understood her.

If Electra could speak well, she could explain the situation. She could keep the United Society for Peace and Strength officers on Eldora Moon from throwing Kor and Khiry in some dark prison and conveniently losing the key.

"Where's Mangor?" the officer in charge barked. It was obvious he wasn't the captain of the vessel. That man had died in the night and this one assumed leadership uncomfortably. "It shouldn't take this long to put a few plasma streams into a few lifeless bodies. I want to lift off this rock before the storm worsens."

He turned to the officer flipping switches and turning dials next to him. "Petters. Go help Mangor. Take one of these bodies with you. I want my bridge cleaned up."

Kor climbed to his feet. "I'll help."

All six eyes at the bridge console looked at him. The acting captain showed trepidation.

"You can trust this man, Captain," Electra said. "He is John Ashley McCormick the third. He and his family have served my family and the United Society for Peace and Strength for generations. He has saved my life many times over already. He is a capable ally in all you need done aboard a ship that's missing so many of her crew."

Khiry recognized more of Electra in that speech than in anything the woman had said yet that day. Maybe being back among USPS officers pulled her back to her true calling.

"I can help with liftoff," Khiry said, climbing to her feet as well.

Electra nodded. "Indeed. This is Khiry Okerson, the pilot and communications officer of the Instigator. She assumed command of that vessel's crew when the captain and security chief committed treason against the United Society for Peace and Strength. She is another capable ally…" Electra's voice trailed away as her gaze shifted to something beyond Khiry, something heavy and ugly moving in rapid, jerking steps up the wide hall toward the bridge.

*   *   *   *   *

Khiry knew that look. It was the look of stark terror. Sometimes, when a person has been pushed to the limit, or when he or she suddenly confronts a mortal fear, the person can freeze. She'd heard it called "petrified." That might be an appropriate description for Electra at the moment. She stood immobile, like one of Medusa's victims caught gazing at the gorgon.

The officer name Petters moved toward Khiry, as if to take hold of her, to protect her.

Khiry spun on her heel, backing toward the advancing Petters. The combination of movements tripped her, sending her clumsily to her backside on the metallic floor as the shape of Gibson in demon form lumbered onto the bridge. Its spittle stank of rancid meat. He'd been feeding on the dead in the sick bay.

Khiry felt her stomach turn. Her throat made an involuntary sound—the sound of sickness.

Gibson looked down at this, shielding his eyes from the light with what looked like part of someone's leg. As if something in his brain retained a memory of her—and not a good one—he reached for her. A stream of plasma removed his arm before he could make contact. His howl filled the ship and he turned his anger on Kor. He moved with superhuman speed, as all the touched did. Behind him, the officer named Mangor wailed through the doorway with unkempt features and bleeding eye sockets. The light obviously distressed these two and Mangor hadn't the presence of mind left to use a tool to protect his eyes.

Kor primed the weapon again and fired through Gibson's body. It split in two main pieces, the torso exploding with the customary gore they'd come to expect from the touched.

Petters reached down to lift Khiry from the floor. While she appreciated the chivalry, she pitied the foolishness. Exposing his head exposed his ignorance of not just the touched's strength, but also their drive and hunger.

Mangor lunged over Khiry and sank his ring of jagged teeth deep through Petters' skull and into his brain. Firing straight up, Khiry blasted Mangor as he dove over her, but she was too late. Petters screamed in panicking death.

Electra's tears nearly blinded her, but she used her own weapon to finish the thrashing officer.

The captain stared in disbelief at the carnage before him. "God, save us," he muttered. "What…"

Electra placed a hand gently on his arm. "It's over now. We'll get back to Eldora Moon and report—"

The man shook his head. "This is insanity. Is this what you've endured on the planet? Is this how those people had to live?"

Electra couldn't bring herself to offer him any sort of smile to soften the blow. "I'm afraid so."

"For years?"

"Yes," she said quietly. "Now you've saved three lives from it. Let's get back to Eldora—"

He stepped away from her, shaking his head more vigorously. From her vantage point in the floor, Khiry swallowed hard. She figured the newly appointed captain was about to have some kind of mental break. Just because you wore an officer's uniform didn't mean you were fit to lead. Not everyone was fit to take a group of intelligent, savvy, trained colleagues and stand over them in a position of authority. No number of medals on his uniform could give him the mental strength he needed for this moment.

When he unholstered his weapon and placed it to his temple, only Electra was close enough to grab it. But

Electra was the least prepared for his action. She emitted a quick, high-pitched shriek as the blast went cleanly through his head. He stood for a second, staring straight into her, accusing her of bringing the United Society for Peace and Strength into a situation that should have stayed neatly on the foreign planet. Then he fell in a heap of gray uniform and red brain matter.

Electra turned to Kor and Khiry. Her eyes sought first Kor's seeing sympathy there. She didn't want sympathy. Next she locked the cool gaze of a leader with Khiry. The young woman pursed her lips and nodded once at Electra. "We have to leave the planet."

Electra agreed, but hadn't found her voice yet. Her diaphragm was too constricted by horror to expand and fill with air. She couldn't push sound up and out.

Khiry looked at Kor. "Will you take these bodies to an airlock? See if Onyx will help you? And get the bodies in the sick bay to the airlock, too?"

"Best plan I've heard since the mess hall," he said, pulling her from the floor.

The lightness of the statement surprised both of them. Khiry almost smiled. Almost. Her eyes met his with a bit of dance to them. "Are we going to Eldora Moon?" she asked.

Electra hadn't considered any other destination, but now let the question seep into her. Kor also seemed to be caught off guard by it. They both watched Khiry for her explanation.

"Gibson was taking these coils to Pangaea for a reason," Khiry suggested. "Good money."

"To supply the jumpers," Kor told her. As if she needed more explanation, he added, "the *resistance,*" with emphasis.

"I'm aware."

Electra had finally caught her breath. "Is anyone here really loyal to the USPS any longer?"

That made Khiry smile. "Never thought I'd hear myself say it, but the USPS can pag themselves right off every planet they're sending people to. They've no regard for who they're sending out to their deaths. If we can sell these coils to the blenders on Pangaea, maybe they can drive the USPS off one rock out here."

Kor shook his head in disbelief. "I agree. Against my better judgment, I agree, and my father and grandfather are no doubt spinning so hard in their graves they're fueling a turbine somewhere. To Pangaea, then?"

Electra felt a swell of pride and purpose rush into her blood. It was warm and soothing. "To Pangaea."

"What of the dragons?" Kor asked.

Khiry looked to Onyx sitting like a sphinx with Junior sobbing quietly between his front claws. The regal black dragon watched her with solemn blue-gray eyes.

"It would be dangerous taking them back to the moon. And I think they'd be willing to journey with us…a while at least."

Kor whistled lightly as he reached for what remained of Gibson's body. As he dragged the heavy mass toward the doorway of the bridge, he said, "I agree again. Stay on guard for anything else strange up here, but let's get moving. I'll get these ready for jettison."

Onyx patted Junior into place near a wall and rose to collect the body of the dead captain. He squeezed down the hallway to follow Kor.

* * * * *

They'd been in hyperdrive several hours before Kor returned to the bridge and flopped into a chair. He swiveled to face Khiry. "Electra's sleeping in the captain's quarters just behind this wall. Junior's with her." He pointed as if she'd not know to which wall he referred.

"That's good. She's under enormous stress."

"Not as much anymore. The ship's clear as best I can tell."

"Not as much? She's just turned her back on her family and all she's ever known to become a rebel against her government."

He chuckled. "When you put it that way…"

She turned back to the controls. "I've never been so paranoid about watching a ship's course before. Electra told me there was a homing beacon on every USPS vessel and we ripped it out."

"Is that it?" He gestured toward two piles of frayed and melted cables in the floor behind her.

She grinned. "Yes."

"So you're saying no one will find this ship?"

"We disabled it, then took it apart and fried the components. Then we melted the wires and cables. The smell bothered Onyx. That's when he went to sleep over there." She nodded her head toward the front of the bridge where the windows joined the bulkhead.

"Again, you're saying no one will find this ship."

Her grin widened. "Electra's the ace up our sleeves. I'm so glad she didn't snap like that captain did."

"He wasn't really a captain."

She sniffed. "He should never have assumed command if he couldn't take it."

He smiled at her, not responding.

After a few minutes of that, she looked over at him. "What?"

"Come here and let me hold you while you fly."

The End

About the Author

Fantasy enthusiasts will recognize Sandy Lender as the author of the breakout novel *Choices Meant for Gods* and a leader of workshops on world-building and characterization.

Her four-year degree in English and seventeen-year career in magazine publishing augment her book publishing experience for a variety of presentations.

She is the author of Choices Meant for Gods, Choices Meant for Kings and What Choices We Made, Volumes One and Two.

Learn more about Sandy at www.authorsandylender.com or www.todaythedragonwins.blogspot.com